Domestic Disturbance

Five Story Collection

Dara Girard

ILORI
Press Books, LLC

Also by Dara Girard

Collections

Dark Love

The Lady Next Door and Other Stories

Holiday Hearts

Lost and Found

5 Holiday Tales

10 Holiday Stories

Duvall Sisters

The Glass Slipper Project

Taming Mariella

A Reluctant Hero

The Black Stockings Society

Power Play

A Gentleman's Offer

Body Chemistry

Round the Clock

Return of the Black Stockings Society

Playing for Keeps

After Hours

A Private Affair

Just One Look

Private Lessons

Ladies of the Pen

Words of Seduction

Pages of Passion

Beneath the Covers

Henson Series

Table for Two

Gaining Interest

Careless Rapture

Dangerous Curves

Familiar Stranger

It Happened One Wedding

Unexpected Pleasure

Midnight Promise

Sweet Temptation

Always and Forever

Clifton Sisters

The Sapphire Pendant

The Amber Stone

The Emerald Ring

Fortune Brothers

A Tempting Proposal

A Seductive Arrangement

An Unforgettable Moment

Novels

Honest Betrayal

The Daughters of Winston Barnett

Remember My Name

Illusive Flame

Winterwood Lane

Best Laid Plans

Piece of Cake

Dream of Me

Introduction

Home is where the heart is...

I love taking phrases and turning them around. In the following stories home is where the heart is broken, shattered and sometimes healed.

This collection starts with "Routines" where a woman searches for her ex-husband and finds out more about herself.

In "The Secret" a young girl tries to guard her family name although it may destroy her.

In "One of A Kind" a woman searches for justice she's not sure she'll ever get.

"Stolen Angel" finds a burglar discovering that her actions have consequences beyond what she'd ever imagined.

And finally "Smoke Screen" is a fantastical story about a woman who is forced to face her past in a dark and sinister way.

I hope you'll enjoy reading these tales as much as I did writing them.

Dara Benton

July 2014

Routines

Routines

It wasn't like James to be late. Lynn Thompson checked her watch for the eighth time, just to make sure. Five after five. Her ex-husband said he'd come and pick up their daughter, Evelyn, at five on the dot. He always said 'on the dot' because he liked precision and didn't like to waste time. He was always on time. To him lost time was like leaving a hundred dollars on a sidewalk. He'd rather write a check for a thousand dollars than to let one minute pass without his knowledge. Schedule was his most favorite word. So she'd expected to hear the quick rap of his knuckles on the door at exactly five o'clock.

But she hadn't heard anything. Not a car driving up or his steady, paced footsteps on the cobblestone path leading to the front door. Twice, she'd looked out the window of her townhouse to see if his car was making its way around the corner. But all she saw were people coming home from work or afterschool programs. There was no sign of his black Toyota.

Lynn glanced at her watch again wondering if she should be annoyed or worried. Someone else would tell her that five minutes was nothing to fuss over. But she knew James Holbrook the third. James was reliable. Predictable. Some would say boring. That was one of the reasons their marriage had ended. There was no spark or surprises left. She knew exactly what he'd eat for break-fast--a boiled egg, buttered toast, two slices of melon--and what he'd watch on Saturdays. She knew that he went to the gym on Fridays and called his ailing mother on Sundays. He never wavered from his routine. Unlike many husbands, he never forgot their anniversary, but always planned the same thing--the same restaurant and gift--a necklace and dinner at the Greek Restaurant off of Third Street.

"What more do you want?" her mother once said when Lynn complained about him. "At least he remembered."

"Like a computer. There's no thought. He just goes through the motions."

And it continued that way. With James seeming to go through the motions of being a husband and her pretending that it was all okay. When their daughter was born, Lynn had expected--hoped for--a shift. But not much changed. He just put their new baby on a regular schedule as well. When Lynn asked for a divorce seven years later, she'd briefly shaken him out of his routine. She still remembered the look of shock on his face. He hadn't expected it. Hadn't sensed her unhappiness. Couldn't understand why she said they'd grown apart.

He'd thought they were perfect together. She told him the marriage was over and why she felt there was nothing they could do. He listened to her quietly as they sat in the kitchen, their daughter asleep upstairs, his gaze steady, with a sad acceptance clear in his eyes. Once she'd finished he nodded and said, "If that's what you want."

It had annoyed her that he'd been so causal about it. So accepting. She'd wanted him to put up a fight of some sort. To show that he cared about his marriage and would fight for it. That he'd change his routines so that there could be something more between them. Instead, he moved out and their trial separation turned into a divorce. However, he kept his routine up with their daughter. He saw her every week and planned a father and daughter trip every month.

Lynn looked at her watch again. Ten minutes after five. She swore. Something was wrong. He should be here. This didn't make sense. One thing he never did was disappoint their nine year old daughter. He'd promised to take her ice skating. James was not one to break a promise. If he was late--which he'd been on only two rare occasions, by seven minutes--he would call. But he hadn't called. He hadn't texted or sent an email to say he had to cancel.

Lynn glanced at her daughter who sat in the living room watching a cartoon on TV.

"Nothing is wrong," she told herself as she dialed his number. "Please don't let anything be wrong." Her call went directly to voice mail. She groaned low in her throat then sent him a text. She stared at the screen silently praying that a reply would instantly pop up.

It didn't.

Lynn started to dial his mother's number then stopped. She didn't want to worry her. It was Friday evening and she knew his mother would already be waiting for her call from him on Sunday. She cherished those calls--lived for them. No, Lynn wouldn't bother his mother about something that could very well be nothing. Lynn went into her kitchen and grabbed a bag of plantain chips. She began munching through each one trying to think of what to do. She'd give him another minute. *Maybe there was traffic.* But he was the type who would let her know, her mind said resisting her attempts to ratio-nalize the situation. *Maybe he had a flat tire.* Again, he would have called. Lynn glanced down at her phone. It wasn't like him to have his calls go directly to voice mail either. He was always available. In case there was some-thing wrong with his mother or daughter she'd always been able to get a hold of him.

When Lynn glanced at her wall clock--a wooden one in the shape of Jamaica--and saw it read five- twenty she knew she needed to do something. She set her bags of chips down and grabbed her keys.

"Come on, let's go," she said to her daughter. She turned off the TV.

Evelyn jumped up in dismay. "But Daddy isn't here yet."

"Exactly," Lynn said zipping up her daughter's coat, trying to stall just in case he called or suddenly arrived.

Evelyn stared at her with wide brown eyes. "Do you think he's hurt?"

Yes. "I don't know, honey," Lynn said determined to keep her voice light. "I have to find out. I'm sure it's nothing." She locked up the house then went to the car. "We'll stop by his office. Maybe he worked late and lost track of time," she said the words, although she didn't think they were true.

"Daddy never loses track of time," Evelyn said getting into the backseat.

I know. That's what worries me, she thought. But she kept her fears to herself.

* * *

"Lynn and Evie what are you doing here?" Maria Rodriguez said as they came off the elevator. She was the office manager and had been since the beginning. James had started the software company fourteen years ago with his Uncle Lewis. Lynn had attended Maria's two baby showers. Lynn hadn't seen her in two years, having no reason to stop by the office after the separation and divorce. She noticed that Maria had lost her once trim figure, but still had her beautiful, smooth olive skin and beaming smile. The office atmosphere still had the feeling of a family as much as a business, it was like she'd never left and nothing had changed.

"We came to see James," Lynn said.

Maria frowned then glanced at Evelyn and fixed her features. "Evie, why don't you go to the kitchen and ask

Kirk to get you some hot chocolate. Okay?" Evelyn nodded then left. Once she was out of hearing, Maria's face grew serious. "What's going on?"

"I don't know. I'm trying to find out."

"James is not here. He told me that he was taking Evie ice skating and he wanted his schedule clear so he could leave on time. Which he did--on the dot."

"So that was about an hour ago?"

"Not about. Exactly."

"Right."

"Where else have you looked?"

"This was the first place I thought of. I didn't want to call anyone else, because I knew they would worry." Lynn rubbed her forehead, feeling the tense grip of a headache. "Do you mind if I look in his office?"

"No, let's go. I'm sure it's nothing."

Lynn forced a smile knowing Maria was trying to lie to them both in order to feel better. She took a deep breath then entered his office. "Does anything look strange?" Lynn asked looking around.

Maria shook her head. "No, everything looks in place."

Lynn agreed. His office and desk were in perfect order. Everything was organized. He was always trying to organize her, too. The kitchen had been pristine. Their bedroom even more so, his side of the room was always done with military precision while she had a tendency to throw her clothes. She picked up the framed photo of Evelyn on his desk. She had some of her father's habits-- her room was always clean and her meals were always arranged with the vegetables on a separate plate. Lynn set the photo down. There were no clues here. *Where are you, you bastard?* She silently wondered, but, unfortunately, he wasn't a bastard. He never had been. He was a genuinely nice guy. He'd created a good business for himself, had a strong family and good friends. She hadn't fit in. That's why their marriage had ended. He'd preferred to keep to his routines than to keep her.

Lynn brushed the thought aside--hating how the failure of her marriage still brought pain-- and opened a drawer. She blinked in surprise when she saw a wallet with Mickey Mouse on the front. She'd bought the wallet for James as a joke on their honeymoon. She hadn't expected him to keep it. She thought he would have thrown it away or donated it. Maybe he'd forgotten. She picked up the wallet and opened it. Inside was a picture of them and the million dollar check she'd made out to him. "You're a million bucks to me," she'd written.

"You found something?" Maria asked curious.

Lynn quickly shoved the fake check into the wallet then tossed the wallet back in the drawer and closed it. "No. I thought I had," she lied. "But it's nothing. Is business going well?"

"Wonderfully. We just got a new client." Maria checked the calendar on her cell phone. "And there's nothing out of the ordinary on his schedule. He seemed in good spirits and didn't act strange in anyway. Too bad we can't go to the police."

"They'd laugh us out of the station," Lynn grimly agreed. He was an adult and they both knew they would have to wait 48 hours before the police even made his disappearance an issue.

"Let me call him," Maria said dialing before Lynn could reply.

Lynn nodded anyway, but knew it would be a wasted effort and it was. Her call went directly to voice mail.

"Today is Friday right?"

"Yes."

"So he'd leave here and do a round at the gym before picking Evie up. So I'll go there."

"Good luck."

"Do you mind dropping Evie at my mother's place?" Lynn gave Maria the address. "I don't want to drag her around with me until I know what's happened."

"No problem."

* * *

IN THE ELEVATOR, Lynn called her ex-brother in law, Ronald. "I need you to stop by James' apartment. He was supposed to pick up Evie and he hasn't shown up."

He laughed. "That's a good one and I just had a date with a supermodel."

"What was her name?"

He paused then swore. "Wait. You're serious?"

His reaction made Lynn's heart twist. He, too, knew this wasn't like James. She fought to keep her voice from trembling. "I'm afraid so. I spoke to Maria and she said he left work on time. We've both tried to reach him, but the calls go straight to voice mail. I'm going to check the gym."

"Okay, I'll go to his place." He didn't tell her that it was probably nothing, because like her he knew that wasn't true.

* * *

"Yes, he was here," the clerk said.

"Did he seem distracted or anything?"

"No, he had a regular workout, but didn't want to chat because he said he was picking up his daughter."

For Evelyn's sake she hoped it was nothing, Lynn thought as she returned to her car. The divorce had been hard enough. She didn't need this. Whatever *this* was. Should she check the hospitals? But if he had been admitted wouldn't they have called his family? Should she go to her social media resources and let others know? It would annoy James, if nothing was wrong, because he hated to be the center of anything and didn't like people fussing over him. But maybe she wouldn't have to. Maybe she'd get a call from his brother and he'd tell her something useful. Ten minutes later the call from Ronald did come, but it wasn't what she wanted to hear.

"Lynn, you need to come over and see this."

"Can't you just tell me over the phone?"

"No, I can't describe it. Get here as soon as you can."

She was there even faster, likely breaking several traffic laws, but, thankfully, no one stopped her. Before she got a chance to knock on the door, Ronald opened it, as if he'd been waiting in the foyer. She prepared herself then stepped inside and paused. The place looked fine. She'd expected something else.

"What's wrong?" she said baffled. "I don't see anything."

"Just wait," he said in a grim voice.

Lynn gripped her hands into fists. "I don't have time for this. Just tell me."

He held up his hand and then a woman came into the room and smiled at them. "Oh, hi. You must be Lynn."

Lynn absently shook the other woman's hand. She was attractive, and fit with a bright smile and cold eyes. "Would you like anything to drink?"

"No, who are you?"

"Carmen. I've been seeing James. Excuse me while I put on some more coffee." She left.

Lynn turned to Ronald and said in a low tone, "You asked me here to see *her*?"

"Yes."

"Why? Does she know where James is?"

He shoved his hands into his pockets. "I haven't asked her yet."

"Why not?"

"Because something doesn't seem right. She's not his type. She's too pretty."

"Oh thanks."

"I mean too perfect. Look at her."

"She seems like she'd be James' equal. He likes things perfect. Organized. In their place." Lynn turned to the door. "Just ask her where she--"

Ronald grabbed her arm and turned her around.

"Stop thinking with your heart and use your head. You know my brother as well as I do. Don't just think of him as your ex. Remember, you'd been friends for years before you got serious. Really look at her and this place. Please."

It was the 'please' that did it. And the look in his eyes. He was truly worried and it mirrored her own fears. She wanted it to be over so she'd been quick to grasp at an apparently easy answer. James had a new girlfriend. That would be a quick, pat solution. "Okay, you enjoy your coffee while I check out the bathroom."

Ronald didn't argue with her. He just nodded as if he trusted that she knew what she was doing. She didn't. She went into the bathroom and stared at her reflection. *What am I supposed to do?* She looked around the room. Nothing seemed out of place. Spotless. Towels placed at an even length. Color coordinated. She checked the medicine cabinet. Nothing spectacular. Just his allergy medicine and aftershave. She took the bottle and opened it. Sometimes she missed that smell. It wasn't the same smelling it from the bottle as it was on his skin. He had his own unique scent. Woodsy, warm, solid. She put the aftershave back and left the bathroom. She returned to the living room where Ronald looked at her with a silent question. She only shrugged before Carmen turned to her with her bright smile and chilly gaze.

"I was just telling Ronald that I don't know where James is. We had an argument and I haven't heard from him. I'm sure once he cools off he'll get in touch with you."

Lynn suddenly became more alert. No matter how angry James got he wouldn't forget to pick up his daughter. She started to study the woman more, taking note of her perfect teeth and carefully chosen words. Lynn watched Carmen refill Ronald's coffee and surreptitiously took a photo of her with her mobile phone, before tucking it away. "How did you meet him?" Lynn asked, hoping her voice sounded casual.

Carmen paused, startled. And Lynn felt glad she'd surprised her out of her practiced responses. "What?"

"How did you meet him?"

"At work."

"Funny how Maria forgot to mention you."

"It wasn't at his office it was in the building. We met on the elevator."

"And just struck up a conversation?"

"Yes."

"About what?"

Her lips thinned. "Does it matter?"

"Shouldn't it? I remember exactly how I met him. At a mechanic shop. He overheard the mechanic overcharge me by two hundred dollars and argued it down to the right price. I then treated him to coffee as a thank you and the rest is history."

"Our meeting wasn't as interesting. Many aren't."

"You're not his type."

Carmen narrowed her eyes. "People change."

"Where is he?"

"I told you I don't know."

"What was your fight about?"

Carmen waved her hand suddenly seeming to relax. "It was something silly."

"How silly?" Lynn asked watching and analyzing her every movement.

"It was about the ketchup bottle."

Lynn froze. "What about it?"

"He hates how I'll add water to make it last longer. It drove--drives--him crazy."

Lynn didn't know how to breathe. They'd argued about that too. He hated when she added too much water or any at all. He'd prefer to leave some ketchup at the bottom and buy a fresh new bottle. But if Carmen knew that about him then it meant that James had been seeing her and perhaps the rest of the story was true. But it couldn't be. He wouldn't have forgotten Evelyn.

"Sorry I couldn't help you with anything else, Lynn."

Lynn gritted her teeth. She hated how Carmen said her name. It grated on her nerves--like spreading marmalade on cardboard--sweet with nothing substantial underneath. Only one other person could do that. But she couldn't think who it was. She looked at Carmen again. Who did this woman remind her of? And why hadn't she mentioned Evelyn? James had mentioned picking up his daughter for ice skating to everyone else, why hadn't Carmen mentioned it? This supposed girlfriend knew something, but wasn't going to share. Lynn had to come up with a new strategy.

She stood. "I'll be back in an hour. I'll talk to James then," she said, then left.

* * *

"She knows something," Lynn said as she and Ronald stood outside the apartment building, the winter wind stinging her cheeks.

"But we can't prove it."

"I don't know why she reminds me of someone." She rubbed her hands together, knowing it wasn't just the weather that made her feel cold. "I'm going to find out what she knows."

"But I don't think she'll break. What do you think she's up to?"

"I don't know."

"James was crushed by the divorce," Ronald said in a low voice.

Lynn sniffed. "How could you tell? Was his tie half an inch off center?"

"No, but I'm just saying that maybe he hasn't handled the divorce as well as he wanted us all to believe. Maybe that woman really is someone he's seeing and he did stormed off in a rage. Maybe he got drunk or--"

"Or maybe he was abducted by aliens," Lynn cut in with a sarcastic tone. "Decided to hitchhike his way to North Dakota. It's not likely. The divorce was hard, but he hasn't changed."

"How do you know?"

"The same way you do. Gut instinct."

"I don't know, Mom said he sounded subdued after their last phone call."

"Recently?"

He nodded.

"That's strange because Maria said he's been the same as always. And let's not forget Evie. No matter what, he's always there for her."

"Then what could it be?"

"What did Mom say?" Lynn asked desperate for any clues. "What were they talking about?"

"She wouldn't say. Just that he seemed upset when he dropped by."

"Unannounced?"

"Yea, that's weird isn't it? He doesn't usually just stop by to see her without letting her know."

"I have to find out why."

* * *

SHE DIDN'T WANT TO, but Lynn knew she would have to see her. Speaking to James' mother over the phone had always been hard. Her West Indian accent was so thick and Lynn wondered what version of English she'd learned: American, British, Australian or a mixture of all three? She was a thin, tall woman who had given her son his exacting ways. Unlike Lynn who had a round figure, quick speech and restless ways, Mrs. Holbrook had a deep voice and deep set eyes. The first time they'd met, they liked each other instantly. Lynn didn't want to worry her, but she needed some questions answered--fast.

Mrs. Holbrook's face lit up when she saw her. "What a surprise. How are you darling?"

"Hi Mom," Lynn said bending down to give her a hug. "I was just in the neighborhood."

"No, you weren't," Mrs. Holbrook said, her keen dark gaze studying her. "What's wrong?"

Damn. "I missed you."

"I missed you too."

"Where's Evie? Oh wait, I remember. James told me he was taking her ice skating."

"Yes, that's right. So I have free time. I heard that James stopped by to see you and I wanted to see you too."

His mother folded her arms and made her face into a pout. "I'm still mad at you for breaking my son's heart."

Lynn laughed, hoping it sounded genuine. "He's moved on. He's seeing a very beautiful lady."

Mrs. Holbrook frowned. "He hasn't told me he's seeing anyone."

Lynn took out her phone and showed her the photo.

"He can't be seeing her. She's gotten her face done."

"How can you tell?"

She tapped the screen. "The job is good, but she's gotten too much done. Her skin doesn't fall right around her jaw line."

Lynn shrugged. If a woman wanted to use plastic surgery to boost her confidence she wasn't one to judge. "I wouldn't have known."

"James would and besides, he likes his ladies natural. There's something familiar about her though."

"I had the same feeling." Lynn put her phone away. "Are you doing well?"

"As well as expected." Mrs. Holbrook rested her hands in her lap and shrugged.

Lynn glanced at her bare hand in surprise. "Where's your ring?"

"I misplaced it. I've been misplacing a lot of things lately."

"Like what?"

"My ruby bracelet, a gold watch."

"And you never find them again?"

"Yes, I do, but James said that he was going to get me a lock box and that I was to put all my things in there. He seemed more upset about my missing things than I was. I was surprised when he visited me only a few days ago. He was very angry about the jewelry. But they're just things and they always turn up again. Lewis thinks James is concerned for no reason and I agree. He took me to dinner."

"James?"

"No, Lewis. He's such a dear younger brother to me. Now, more than ever."

Uncle Lewis had started visiting her? He hadn't done that when she and James were still married. His Uncle lived for work and women, rarely having time to stop by and see his sister. Although he did send flowers and chocolates.

"Has anyone else had things go missing?"

"No, just me. But like I said, they find their way back. I was so glad when I got my pearl necklace back."

"Do you mind?" Lynn asked gesturing to the jewelry case."

"Go ahead."

Lynn looked in Mrs. Holbrook's jewelry case and pulled out the pearls. Good fakes, but fakes all the same. She now knew why James had been upset, she was too. Someone was stealing his mother's jewels. Had James stumbled upon a large theft ring going on in the nursing home and gotten into trouble? But why just Mrs. Holbrook's jewels and no one else's?

Lynn chatted with Mrs. Holbrook a little more then left with more questions than answers.

As she walked down the hallway she glanced at the many photographs of the residents and staff. Then one image caught her attention. She saw the cold eyes in a dowdy, hangdog face. The woman was twenty pounds overweight, dressed in shapeless clothes. But the cold eyes were distinctive. Carmen. Now Lynn knew why the other woman seemed so familiar. Where she'd remembered her from. She'd been one of the nurses. How had she been able to afford major plastic surgery? An inheritance, perhaps? Or marrying well? There hadn't been any recent stories of a young woman marrying an older, wealthy man on his death bed, but it could have happened. He wouldn't have been a resident at this facility, but maybe she'd become a private nurse. Maybe she was a wealthy widow. Had she and James fallen in love during one of his visits to see his mother?

Lynn went to the front desk and pointed to the picture. "Whatever happened to her? My mother would like to send her a note of thanks."

"I'm afraid she can't."

"Why not?"

"Because she died last year."

WELL ONE THING she knew for sure was that Carmen wasn't dead. She'd had some work done and was now pretending to be James' girlfriend. They may have gotten close while she worked at the nursing home, but why would she fake her death and where had she gotten the money to do the plastic surgery? Who was stealing Mrs. Holbrook's jewelry and why? What had James uncovered and had it cost him his life? Lynn shook herself out of the thought and hurried to her car then her phone alerted her. She looked down and saw a text.

Sorry I missed picking up Evie. I'm okay. Talk later.

Lynn felt a growing rage. James would never text her. He would call. She would let this intruder know about his or her deception. The police are looking for you. It was a lie, but she wanted whoever was involved to feel the pressure. To stop playing this bizarre game with her. Tell me where you are.

She didn't expect a reply and didn't receive one. But Lynn knew now that two things had changed. James visiting his mother, instead of calling and Uncle Lewis showing his sister special care, when he rarely had before.

Only one person would make James change his routine. Someone he trusted. Between the gym and her house something had changed. Something, or someone, had taken him off track and she was beginning to think she knew who.

"DID YOU FIND ANYTHING?" Ronald asked when he opened the door of his house to let Lynn in.

Lynn shook her head and stepped inside. She didn't know how to tell him about the fake jewels or the nurse. She headed for the family room then stopped when she saw a picture of a wedding--Uncle Lewis with Carmen *before* the surgery.

She yanked the picture from the wall and gripped it in her hands, trying to comprehend what she was seeing. A dowdy younger woman with a much older man. "What's this?"

"Oh, Uncle got married to Cecile about two years ago. Happened when you and James were separated otherwise I'm sure you would have been there. No one thought the old bachelor would ever get hitched, but he did. They met at the nursing home."

"I know," Lynn said in a hollow voice amazed at the cold gaze that stared back at her. "I remember her."

"You met her too?"

"Yes." Cecile...yes she remembered her.

"She was sweet and they were perfect together."

Lynn didn't remember her being sweet. The woman she'd met was nosy and bossy. Lynn felt like she was always listening to their conversations. She almost sensed a jealousy. Yes, now she remembered that she and James had mentioned their silly ketchup argument with Mrs. Holbrook and later had a good laugh. That was how Cecile--now Carmen--could pretend to know James. But what was she doing at his place?

"They were only married six months before the accident that took her life. Uncle couldn't function after that--couldn't sleep, wouldn't eat and James was worried about him at work. So he came to live with us."

Lynn stared at Ronald surprised. "He's here now?"

"Yes, we made up a room for him. Wait...where are you going?"

"To get some answers." Lynn marched in the direction Ronald had gestured to. She stopped in front of the door and banged on it.

"What answers?" Ronald said hurrying behind her. "What could Uncle Lewis know?"

"We'll see." She knocked again. "Uncle Lewis I need to talk to you."

The door opened. He smiled at her. Unlike Carmen it was his smile that chilled her. "Lynn, what a pleasant--"

Lynn held up her hand. "Cut the crap. Where is he?"

He frowned. "What?"

"Take me to him now."

"Take you to whom?" he asked stumbling over the words.

"James."

Ronald took a step forward, his voice filled with apology. "Uncle, she's upset because James was late and--"

"He knows why I'm here," Lynn said. "And you have one minute to tell me where he is."

Ronald took her arm. "I don't think--"

Lynn snatched her arm away. "He knows everything. Where is James?"

Uncle Lewis shook his head. "I don't--"

Lynn pushed past him, grabbed a pair of scissors off a side table then opened his closet and saw a row of fine suits. "Still have expensive taste. Now start talking."

"I don't know---

Lynn sliced through the back of one of the suits. "Does that help your memory?"

"What is wrong with you?" he cried.

She took the sleeve of another suit. "Do I really have to do this?"

"I told you I don't--wait...okay. All right." He held up his hands in surrender. "You win."

Ronald stared at him stunned. "Uncle?"

"How much do you know?"

"Enough. I know that your wife isn't dead. Ronald and I saw her in James' apartment today. A lot of her has changed, but that voice and those eyes were a giveaway. Then there was your sister's fake jewelry. What's the story? James discovered your fraud didn't he? "

"I told him to let it go," he said with a heavy sigh. "I told him that it was none of his business. That it was best to ignore it."

"But he wouldn't let it go."

"No. When I fell in love with Carmen I promised her the world. The business was doing well and I was lonely and things were great. Then she wanted to get a few things done to her face and body and I was fine with that.

Then came the shopping sprees, but I didn't worry about them too much at first. I felt like a lucky man having such a beautiful woman. But then soon it wasn't enough. I only meant to take one of Minnie's jewels, just to cover a few expenses then things got out of control and I took some money from the business accounts. The insurance fraud was Carmen's idea. She had an insurance policy and we were able to fake the right documents with the help of a friend in the coroner's office. We were going to wait a few months then both start new lives. I'd replace some of the money and no one would know."

"But something went wrong."

"Yes. She got cocky after her last surgery. Few people knew who she used to be. She came by the office and James recognized her. He mentioned the jewels and I explained everything. I didn't see it as a big deal. We'd pawn them, but buy them back and eventually return them. I said that I did it for the business. That we needed the money because of the funds I'd taken out. But he threatened to go to the police."

"So what did you do?"

He hung his head and his voice broke. "I didn't mean to do anything." He lifted his gaze to hers. "It was an accident. I just wanted to talk to him."

Lynn's heart froze at the tone of his words. The finality of them. It was too late to realize that she still loved James. That she wished she had tried harder to keep the marriage going. That it wasn't his fault that the marriage had ended and that she needed to take some of the blame. A marriage was a like a hammock. It needed two trees to hold it up or it was useless. It was too late to admit that she missed his reliability, his steady presence, his organization. His love.

"Where is he?"

* * *

THEY FOUND him on the side of an embankment. Lewis and Carmen had gone to James' place to convince him not to go to the police. Lewis and James had gotten into an argument. He'd fallen and hit his head hard. The two of them panicked and put his body in the trunk of his car and dumped his body here. Then Carmen had gone back to James' place to clean up. That's what she'd been doing when Ronald found her, and she had come up with a story to cover her real intentions.

Lynn and Ronald, along with the police, found James where Lewis and Carmen had left him. Wrapped in a plastic sheet, blood frozen to the side of his head. Lynn fell beside his body, wishing she'd found him sooner. Wishing her timing could have been as exacting as his had been. She didn't know what she would tell Evie, but she'd come up with a good story. She'd let her know that her father had been a good, moral man. One who tried to protect those he loved. And they had loved him. She took his cold hand and quietly said goodbye. Then the body made a sound. She quickly checked for a pulse. It was faint but it was there. "Call an ambulance. He's still breathing."

* * *

THE DOCTORS CALLED IT A MIRACLE. James had suffered massive swelling of the brain, but the cold weather had helped slow down the bleeding and trauma to his body. He was released three days later. His Uncle Lewis and his wife were charged with attempted murder and a host of other charges.

Two weeks later, James came to her office. "You should be resting," Lynn said surprised, but happy to see him.

"Ronald told me that you were the one who found me. I wanted to thank you."

She brushed it aside. "You know there's no need for that."

He hesitated then said. "Yes, there is. Can I treat you to a cup of coffee?"

Their relationship had started over a cup of coffee perhaps it could heal that way too. "That would be nice."

He lifted a sly brow. "How about dinner?"

"Even better."

"Saturday. I'll pick you up at six."

Lynn smiled.

"What?" he asked intrigued by the smile.

"You forgot to say 'on the dot.'"

He shook his head, a grin tugging the corner of his mouth. "No, I didn't. I don't have to say that anymore."

"Why not?"

"Because I know if I'm late, you'll come find me."

The Secret

The Secret

THE SECRET WANTED A VOICE. ROBYN FOX SAT IN the front pew of the church, her black, patent leather shoes polished, her braided hair pulled back and clipped with a satin pink bow, and tried to keep her eyes focused on the pastor. He was a tall, charismatic young man brimming with passion, pounding the pulpit with his fiery delivery. Lighting the church up with his heated words, his piercing gaze and love of the Lord.

Robyn struggled to keep still in her seat. She didn't want to make her mother angry. She hated when her mother got angry, it always made Robyn cry. But she wanted to be good today-- *especially* today when it was the assistant pastor's first solo ministry without the senior pastor, and he was talking about heroes who'd lost their lives in wars and America's Independence Day. Robyn bit her lip. She'd been taught to stay silent in church, to just listen or sing, but the secret nearly made her cry out. It urged recognition. It demanded attention. But it was too soon and not the right place. No one could know about it. And she had been good for so long she didn't want to make her mom angry, not now.

You're always doing something wrong, her mother said so many times that Robyn had grown numb to hearing the phrase. She tried hard to be a good girl like the others, but she always made her mother unhappy. Robyn continued to bite her lip as she sat up straight in the front pew, until it bled and a moan escaped her. Her mother nudged her and sent her a hard, dark look of warning. *Don't you dare embarrass me,* the look said. And she didn't want to. She didn't want to shame her.

For a moment the secret fell silent and Robyn licked the blood from her lip, tasting its saltiness. Funny how much blood didn't taste like tears, she thought swinging her legs a little then stopping when she remembered she had to keep still. She lifted her gaze and looked at the church's grand colorful stained windows and vaulted ceiling feeling small. The pastor said God loved all his children, but she wasn't sure she always believed that. She wasn't really pretty or smart, although she tried to be. She tried to keep her grades up, and be polite, but the teacher ignored her when she raised her hand in class and only called on her when she didn't know the answer. Robyn knew that Amanda Wilson was the teacher's favorite and she knew why. Amanda was perky and sweet while Robyn was big and stocky, like all the women on her father's side, with skin the color of roasted coffee beans.

The secret gripped her once again and Robyn

grabbed the pew seat and pressed her legs together. It wasn't time for the secret yet. Her mother said it wasn't for another month and her mother knew everything.

Robyn looked around wondering the best way to escape. She had to get out. She'd been able to hide the secret and she couldn't shame her family. Not when she'd waited so long. She hadn't even been able to acknowledge the secret, her mother slapping her hand away from her expanding middle every time Robyn absently touched it in wonder and fear. When the secret moved inside or kicked her, she had to pretend it wasn't there. It was easy for her family to ignore it because it didn't cling to them everywhere they went, they could deny its presence. She'd tried to do that too at first, pretending that it hadn't happened. That none of it had happened. She was really good at pretending . And it had been so easy at first--that she'd almost convinced herself she was all right. That it wasn't true, but soon pretending didn't help.

Soon pretending seemed silly. Especially, when her favorite Lucky Girls shirt wouldn't fit anymore. They were her favorite singing group and she used to dance to their music in her bedroom, but soon even that became hard. Then her mother wouldn't let her play with her friends anymore. She missed several birthday parties and sleepovers and the fifth grade dance.

She was a big girl, so her mother wasn't too worried about others knowing. She'd fed her more so that she could blame the weight gain on her eating. At first, Robyn hadn't been able to keep anything down, food the one thing that had been a comfort, turning her stomach at the oddest times.

The secret had changed everything that one Wednesday morning at breakfast. She'd bounded down the steps and dashed into the kitchen ready to eat toast smothered with marmalade, hash browns and eggs, but the moment her mother handed her the plate she'd felt her stomach heave.

"You going to be sick?" her older sister, Leena asked. She was thirteen and Robyn hoped to be just like her one day.

Robyn shook her head unsure. She didn't feel sick. At least she hadn't until that moment. She reached for a slice of toast and her insides turned. She gagged and covered her mouth.

Her mother pounded the table. "Don't you dare get sick at my table."

She swallowed hard and pushed herself away.

"Have you been feeling sick long?" Leena said in a softer tone, but her voice had an urgency Robyn didn't understand.

"She's fine," her mother cut in. "Probably a stomach bug."

"But Mom--"

"Shut up and get your sister some ginger tea to settle her stomach."

But Leena didn't move, she just continued to stare at her and Robyn saw her sister's beautiful wide brown eyes, slowly fill with tears. Robyn shifted her gaze to her mother and the look in her mother's eyes tapped down her nausea like an iron fist. The look scared her.

"I said go," her mother said when Leena still didn't move.

Two days later, her sister had Robyn peeing on a stick and that night she heard her mother and sister shouting. Robyn stayed hidden behind the door and watched them in the hallway

"Look what he did to her!" Leena shouted waving the stick.

"Keep your voice down."

Leena made a move to walk past her. "I'm calling the police."

Her mother shoved her back. "No you won't."

"You have to make him leave," her sister shouted.

"I can't. You shouldn't have done this."

"She's only ten. We have to do something."

"You had no right--"

"You're lecturing me?" Leena's voice cracked in disbelief. "Why won't you shout at him? Why didn't you stop this? I'm going to tell--"

Her mother seized her shoulders. "You won't breathe a word of this to anyone."

"I stayed quiet too long. Let go of me."

Robyn saw them struggle then disappear out of view, seconds later she heard the thud. She came out of her room and saw her sister lying on the ground.

Her mother spun around and said, "She fell and hit her head."

Robyn rushed over to her. "Come on, Leena." She

patted her face. "Leena?" She looked up at her mother, her heart racing. "Mom, she's not waking up. Leena!"

Her mother yanked Robyn to her feet. "It was an accident."

"We have to call--"

"No," her mother shouted. She pointed at Robyn, her voice dripping with a quiet fury. "This is your fault. So to make up for it, you'll do exactly what I say...."

And that night she was told to keep two secrets. But that wasn't hard. She was used to keeping secrets, but lying about Leena had been hard, telling people she'd run away instead of saying she'd gone to be with the Lord. Robyn felt her sister deserved more, but knew she couldn't go against her mother. The secret her sister uncovered, had frightened her at first, but soon it became her protection. It protected her from him coming into her room at night, hurting her with his love. She no longer had to worry about him looking at her, he didn't do that anymore.

The secret bit into her, pain shimmering through her middle and down her legs. She bit her lip and squeezed her eyes shut. She felt another hard jab from her mother's elbow. But welcomed that pain compared to the one that gripped her. "I don't feel well," she whispered.

Her mother kept her gaze straight ahead."The sermon's almost over."

But she wasn't sure the secret could wait. She had to defy her mother. Just like Leena. She had to get out of there before anyone knew. She knew her mother would be angry, but she was always angry at her. Angry that it happened. As if it was her fault. "Please, I wanna go home."

"Sit still. We'll go after everyone's left."

The secret pressed down hard and then released her again. Robyn blinked back tears. She missed her dad. Her dad was a warrior--a hero, fighting overseas to help others gain their freedom. He'd told her that she was his little warrior too and she must listen to her mother and follow orders without questions. That's what a good soldier did. Leena hadn't been a good soldier. Her father used to joke that Leena was best suited for the circus, a place where she could make her own rules. Leena hadn't minded. Her sister would do cartwheels and backflips and make funny voices to make him laugh. They used to laugh a lot together. But because Leena hadn't listened, things had gone wrong. She'd heard her father crying, when he'd come home briefly for a visit, and her mother had told him Leena had run away. That's why she had to listen to her mother about keeping the secret. She had to guard her father's good name. Just like a soldier did. She didn't want to make him cry too.

She wanted him to be proud of her. Even though at times she was jealous. Jealous of those people he fought for, when she wished he was home with them. Things were different when he was home. She always felt safe then. She remembered him tucking her into bed and reading her stories. It wasn't like when Andre tucked her in and then got into the bed with her. It felt so wrong, but he told her not to tell anyone, even though each night he hurt her. He was the head of the house when their father was gone.

She prayed for her father to come home to stay. To protect her. But she had to be a good soldier, she couldn't distract him. He had a bigger fight protecting kids fleeing bombed villages, and starving in the desert, her life was better than theirs.

Robyn loved when she got to see him online, telling him how much she missed him, that she wanted to be with him and he'd ask her about school and she'd tell him, but she couldn't tell him what she really wanted to. That she was scared. Did soldiers ever get scared?

The rolling pain washed over her again and this time she gripped the side of her stomach and groaned, doubling over.

"Don't you embarrass me," her mother said.

But the secret didn't care about shame, or embarrassment, or fear, the secret didn't want to stay hidden anymore. Robyn felt her breathing constrict as the pain ripped through her faster and faster, sweat beading on her forehead. She'd told her mother that morning that she didn't want to go to church, that she didn't feel well. But her mother hadn't believed her. She never seemed to believe her. She hadn't believed her when she told her that her sister had been cutting herself, that her brother Andre was hurting her. She didn't lie, but her mother treated her like a liar anyway. So she got into the car, with a dull ache in her back, she'd even had to force a smile at Mrs. Womack, their neighbor, who'd greeted her. She'd always greeted her, once calling her pretty like her dad did, though no one else would.

"It hurts," she whimpered.

"You keep it in. You do that for me."

But she felt as if the secret was killing her, tearing her up inside. She'd seen a horror film once where an alien had ripped through a man's stomach and at that very moment, she felt the same way. The secret had taken over her body. It had taken complete control. But she wanted control back. She didn't want to die like Leena. She didn't want the secret to win. She wanted to see her father again when he came home. She stared at her brother looking so handsome and striking on the pulpit. So powerful. Her mother said that the secret was for him. That he had a bright future. That he carried Dad's name as well, and she had to protect it.

Through a liquid haze of tears, she saw the light shining behind him, the stain glass window casting a rainbow colored glow around him, making him appear like an angel. As though God had touched him with a hand of favor. But Robyn didn't know this man--the one everyone praised and revered. She only knew the man who came in the darkness. Who made her keep secrets.

But she didn't want to keep secrets anymore. She wanted the secret out. She wanted to be free of it, to release it as much as it wanted to be free. She no longer wanted to be afraid of the dark, to sleep curled up under the blankets, to lie to her dad.

Robyn felt her mother take her arm, trying to lift her up, but it was too late now. The secret was coming and just as her mother hadn't protected her all those nights, this time she was going to lose. She saw her mother's eyes widen in horror and rage, but for the first time Roby didn't care. She would soon be free. She bared down hard and screamed out her agony, letting her secret leave the darkness within her and emerge into the light.

One of a Kind

One of a Kind

HE PROBABLY DIDN'T THINK SHE KNEW ABOUT THE other woman, a nurse named Mimi with long legs and a Guyanese accent. *It's a woman's job to keep a man,* her favorite aunt used to say every time she celebrated an anniversary with her third husband. *Catching a man is easy, keeping him is hard. Don't ever take a man's attention for granted.* Amber never did. She liked men. She had a wonderful father who doted on his family. A man who laughed easily and worked hard. She'd married a man similar to her father in temperament, only being with him for three years before cancer took him away. Amber treasured her marriage. It had been perfect.

Her friend, Una laughed at her and called her naive. "All men cheat," Una said.

"Not Hugh," Amber said with a deep knowing.

But Una would just shake her head, her knowing gaze saying 'He just didn't live long enough for you to find out.' But Amber didn't believe that. She didn't believe she was naive, she didn't believe she was blind. Hugh had been her best friend for two years before they married. He'd been at her best friend Cathy's wedding, and she remembered that he didn't smile, which wasn't like him. It was only later that she found out why.

Amber lit the candles and looked around the furnished beach house, the cry of a seagull could be heard in the distance, a sinking sun sending a golden glow across the living room. Bill would be coming over tonight and she'd make sure they had a truly special evening. She remembered when Cathy first introduced them saying he was amazing and one of a kind. Amber had been impressed by the pre-med student's quick wit and charming grin. He'd made a handsome groom standing by Cathy's side at the church. Amber had been the proud matron of honor. She'd wanted her friend to be happy. At the time, she'd only been married two years when she'd watched her friend become a bride too, and still felt like a giddy newlywed.

Cathy hadn't known kindness. Her father loved her, but only when he was sober and that hadn't been frequent, and her mother's three jobs made her a virtual stranger to her children. "I can't wait to have my own little family," Cathy used to say when she came over to Amber's house to study while they were in college "And I'll always be there for my children," she said.

But soon after the wedding she saw her friend change. The change had been gradual and at first, Amber thought it was just the adjustment of becoming a wife and mother.

Things change when women have kids, Amber's mother told her. But Amber knew her mother's words were really an overt hint for her to get over Hugh and move on and make her a grandmother, and not an analysis of her changed friendship. But she wasn't in a rush to get into another relationship and she wasn't convinced that Cathy's two babies had changed things.

Amber checked her braised chicken and roasted asparagus baking slowly in the oven, the glow of the sun waning. Bill had a healthy appetite--not just for food. She still remembered the hot August afternoon after visiting her sister in the hospital, her sister had had a C-section, she'd seen Bill in a lip lock with Mimi in the hospital parking lot. She'd ducked behind a pillar, then peeked her head out just to make sure. Wanting to be wrong, but a sinking feeling in her stomach told her she wasn't. The handsome, six foot doctor was making his rounds in ways her friend never knew. She felt ill and took out her cell phone to call her friend then stopped when a distant memory flashed through her mind.

"Men cheat," Cathy said agreeing with Una's statement. "If mine ever does, I just don't want to know. It's better not to know."

Amber swore and put the cell phone away. As much as she wanted to do something her friend had already told her what to do--nothing. She wouldn't tell her.

She hadn't planned to become his mistress. She knew few people would believe that, but it was the truth. The opportunity had fallen in her lap. After Hugh's death, Bill became a challenging enigma to her. She wasn't used to being around a man who was one way with his family and acted another with strangers. She'd caught his attention at the holiday barbecue, it had been two years into her friend's marriage and a year after Hugh's death. She'd sent him an inviting look as she sipped a cool glass of sorrel juice, half expecting him not to reply. But he did. Faster than she'd planned. They were in bed together within a week. He was a sloppy lover, but that wasn't what she wanted him for.

He probably didn't think Amber knew about the bruising. She'd caught sight of them when Cathy had come over to Amber's house for a brief visit with her youngest. She'd dismissed Amber's questions of concern and said she'd bumped into a wall. But Amber knew the former college track star wasn't that clumsy. They'd been best friends for ten years and loved each other. People wrote love songs, but mostly about romantic love, rarely about the enduring love of friendship, a bond that buries itself deep into the recesses of the heart. Cathy had been her rock when Hugh was sick, preparing meals, and wiping her tears.

Bill didn't care much about their friendship. He wouldn't have jumped in bed with her so easily if he had. Amber didn't think he really liked women or respected them. He just knew how to get them. He was stupid to think she was with him for any other reason than to conduct an experiment. But, if he hadn't been so arrogant, manipulating him wouldn't have been as easy.

He probably didn't think Amber knew about Cathy's fractured ribs and split lip. That her friend had become secretive and taciturn. That she laughed too hard when a joke wasn't funny. That she said his name over and over in a conversation, as if he could rise up like a god any where she went.

Cathy had told her what to do if her husband cheated, but she hadn't given Amber instructions for a man who beat her. Bill shouldn't have touched her friend. He shouldn't have trapped her in a mansion and given her expensive clothes to cover the blue and black marks he left on her body, and draped her in jewelry that glittered on her fingers and neck to divert attention from the sparkle that had left her eyes. Within five years he'd beaten the spirit out of her. The police said it was depression that drove Cathy to take a large a dose of poison that put her in a coma.

He'd cried the night the ambulance took her away. He'd called Amber in a near panic, wailing about being a single father, not knowing what he'd do without her. Amber had given him the comfort he sought, with her body, while her mind drifted elsewhere. Now remembering why Hugh hadn't smiled at Cathy's wedding. Why, as he lay in the hospital room with his eyes sunken in, his breathing shallow, he'd said he wished he didn't have to leave her. That she was naive. "Don't be too trusting. Look after Cathy." He'd understood their friendship. He was never threatened by it. He'd called them sisters of the heart.

But she wasn't naive or blind. She looked helpless and innocent, but that was just a mask. A mask that hid her despair and rage that Hugh was gone, and that Cathy clung to life while the world kept spinning as if nothing had changed.

Amber glanced at the chocolates she'd placed on the table. Bill wouldn't be able to taste what she'd added as he sunk his teeth into his favorite caramel crunch. He wouldn't last too long. She'd have one too, just to divert suspicion. The effects would be unpleasant, but worth it, besides she wouldn't swallow it. This is what a woman did for love, for friendship.

She heard his car drive up and smiled. He was right on time.

He probably didn't know that Amber knew he'd gone to a divorce lawyer and asked about custody of the kids and how much of the estate he'd get to keep.

He probably didn't know that she knew he'd staged the failed suicide attempt. That Amber knew Cathy, no matter how depressed, wouldn't have left her eighteen month old son crying in his high chair while she overdosed in another room. That she wouldn't let her body be found by her five year old when she came home from school. He probably didn't know that Amber knew he'd used his medical knowledge to time the attempted murder well so that he'd never be suspected, and that he'd used her as his alibi. Trying to make her an accomplice just in case anything went wrong, thinking that he could use their affair as a way to manipulate her.

But he didn't know that she'd started the affair to see what kind of man he was, to understand his charm, his hold over her friend, and the illusion he built around his life. To understand how best to get rid of him. She'd never met a man like him. She remembered telling him that one night as they lay in bed and he'd smiled as if she'd complimented him.

Amber greeted him at the door with a kiss. Yes, Cathy was right. Bill was one of a kind--the kind of man the world no longer needed.

Stolen Angel

Stolen Angel

NANCY LOWELL PROMISED HERSELF IT WOULD BE the last time. Not because she'd almost gotten caught, she was too good for that, but because she was getting bored. At forty-something she thought her burglary days were coming to an end, even though she knew she had a few more years left. She was still in excellent shape--the job required it--and loved the thrill of possible discovery, and her team (which consisted of a longtime buddy who helped her find her marks) kept her on her toes. But she felt stuck in a rut. And she knew that luck had a funny way of running out on you. She'd been in the business since she was ten, when her father had taught her all that he knew, which she learned soon enough wasn't much. He was great at making things disappear--jewels, cars, paintings, but he did the same with money, too. They'd get a great stash and in weeks all the money was gone and they were on the lookout again. She ran her business differently. She knew how to make money last.

One last time, Nancy reminded herself as she expertly disabled the security system and waltzed past the gates into the house. She'd hit this house before about a year ago and it had been an easy mark. She knew the cameras were dummies and the security was all on one software she could hack. The Virginia neighborhood smelled of money and privilege. She never caused much alarm in these types of neighborhoods, because what she took was rarely noticed until later. Once inside, she saw that the house was nicely furnished, although overly ostentatious for her taste. She went directly to the places where people usually hide their jewels; inside lingerie drawers, shoe boxes, and the most obvious, jewelry boxes; she also checked the bookshelf for fake books and found one. She opened it and took out the diamond earrings inside. Then she turned to leave. She paused when she heard a car drive up. Damn. Fortunately, she still had time to escape. She quickly cleaned up and zipped up her pouch, but did so too quickly and her penlight slipped out, dropped to the floor, and rolled under the bed.

She saw it and reached for it and her jacket sleeve got caught on the bedspring. She tugged but it wouldn't budge. She heard the front door slam and footsteps. She swore again and tugged harder and heard the cloth tear but not loosen. She didn't have time to take it off. Her only option was to get under the bed when she heard footsteps hit the landing.

"You're such an asshole," a female voice said coming into the room.

"Keep your voice down. The kids--"

"Don't tell me about my kids. The kids you tried to take from me. You think I wouldn't find you? You think I wouldn't show up?"

"Let's not talk about this."

"We'll talk about it now."

"You said you wanted another chance and I'm giving you one."

"Then where's my necklace?"

"I told you I don't know where it is."

"You know I wanted to wear it tonight. I didn't lose it so you must have. Or did you give it to some floozy?"

The man's voice sounded tired. "I don't know where your necklace is and for the fiftieth time I'm not seeing anyone."

"That's what you would say even if you were."

"But I'm not. You're the only woman in my life. And I care about my kids."

"Our kids. The ones you tried to steal."

He sighed. "You're upset. Do you want a bath?"

"No. Don't touch me."

"I'll buy you another necklace."

Nancy silently swore. She remembered that necklace. Didn't think it would cause this kind of trouble. She never thought about her marks.

"I don't want another one. Damn, you're so stupid."

"Let me--"

Nancy heard a slap. She wasn't sure who'd done the action and who'd been hit. There was nothing she could do about it.

"See what you made me do," the woman said. "I told you not to touch me. Don't walk away from me!"

"Let's talk about this in the morning."

"I want to talk now."

Nancy poked her head out and saw the woman pick up a metal statue. She couldn't warn the man as it came down on his head. He stumbled forward. "I hate you!" the woman said.

He spun around and grabbed the statue. He yanked it from her. She whacked him with her purse and then punched him. Nancy noticed a bruise on his cheek. He shoved his wife back and she hit the wall.

She laughed up at him. "What are you going to do, hit me? I'll charge you with abuse."

"Like last time?"

"I'll get the house and the kids and leave you with nothing. No one will believe you. What, you a big strong man can't take care of your woman? Is that why you ran? You thought you could get rid of me? I'll never let you go. You belong to me. Those kids do too and if you ever try to leave me again, I'll make you sorry."

Nancy silently wished he'd slap the smile off her face. Punch it. She'd never been one for violence but the taunting look on the woman's face disgusted her. What kind of woman threatened to hurt her kids? Hit a man and then threatened to call the police? *Leave her*, she wanted to say. *Take the kids and leave. Someone will believe you,*she wanted to say, but she didn't know his situation and knew that few would understand the ugliness he lived with. Domestic violence was still a woman's battle with men as the victimizers, few would sympathize with him. It wasn't her place. And he had tried to leave and she'd found him and she might find him again.

The man calmly put the book back, as a trail of blood leaked from the gash in his head and down his forehead.

The woman watched him and something in her face changed. She crumbled into tears. "I'm sorry. I didn't mean it." She ran up behind him and wrapped her arms around his waist, pressing her cheek against his back. "I love you so much. The thought of you leaving tears me apart. I don't have anyone else but you. You're the only man who's ever loved me; ever been kind to me. Please believe that I'm sorry honey." She walked in front of him. "That cut looks bad, come let me help you." She took his hand and led him to the bathroom.

"I'm fine," he said in a grim tone. "I can do it myself." The sound of rushing water followed.

"Please, don't be angry,"

"Just leave me alone."

The woman began to wail and pleaded with him, closing the door behind her.

Nancy took the opportunity to yank her sleeve free and leave. But not before first replacing the earrings. The man didn't need any more drama than he had. She reached the back door to freedom and grabbed the door handle.

"Can you take me with you?" a little voice said.

Nancy spun around and saw a little girl, about three, holding a doll. She glanced towards the stairs where raised voices continued to be heard. They wouldn't even hear her, but she still kept her voice low.

"You should be in bed," Nancy said.

"I can't sleep. You can help me. Can I come?"

"Shh...no I'll come back for you."

"And my brother too?"

"Yes, now go to bed. And don't tell anyone about me."

"Okay," the little girl said, but she didn't move.

"Now go to bed or your mother will get mad."

The girl sighed. "Mommy's always mad."

* * *

THE CHILD'S words echoed in her mind. Nancy hated lying to the kid, but she'd had to. She hated the thought of the child waiting for her to return, but there was nothing she could do. Nancy looked at the necklace. She hadn't hawked it and didn't know why. She wanted to give it back, but she knew that would only help a little. She wanted to forget about the ugliness in that house. It wasn't her fault that he'd married a banshee. But the big eyes of the little girl waiting to be rescued continued to haunt her.

"It's not your problem," her friend Sally said.

"I know." But she felt responsible. How many other relationships had been altered because of her? What if she hadn't taken the necklace?

"They would be fighting about something else. A rich man who lets his wife beat him, that's just pathetic."

"What if the roles had been reversed? The man

hitting the woman with a book? Punching her in the face?"

"But it wasn't different."

"Abuse is abuse no matter the gender."

"I don't need a lecture. There's nothing you can do. If he won't leave then that's his choice."

"She found him."

"Then he didn't hide very well."

Her friend was right, but Nancy still felt sorry for him. She didn't want to mention how her own mother had belittled her father every day. She wore his smiles down under the heel of her criticisms and caustic remarks until they never emerged again. She and he used to look at the houses they would hit and envy all the glamour, imagining how they could be like the families inside. They envied the fact that there were presents under the Christmas tree, and that some of the families actually sat and ate together, around the dinner table. Her mother didn't have the time. She didn't really care. Her father had once had a favorite model car collection. One day her mother sold it, she said so that she could buy dinner. "Besides, it was just a stupid toy," she said.

FOR TWO DAYS Nancy followed the man--Pete D'Arcy. He looked the picture of success in his expensive car and tailored suits. *No one knows the hell you live in,* Nancy thought, watching him lunch with business associates. He looked jovial and carefree. What a lie you live. Funny how she and her father never thought of that when they imagined the lives that existed in the different houses. They always imagined lives better than theirs--as if privilege somehow eradicated human vices, human suffering. Nancy watched Mr. D'Arcy stop at a jewelry store and silently swore in disgust. Another necklace wouldn't work. She knew that his wife had softened in the last several days. Twice she saw the wife run to his car when he returned from work and kiss him like a newlywed and show him something she'd bought him. It was in a bag so Nancy couldn't see what, but Pete seemed pleased.

Why don't you leave again? She wanted to ask him. Why are you letting her treat you this way? Why would a gift be enough to apologize for a beating? Why did you let her back into your life? Your children's lives? She tried not to feel disdain for him. Although it helped, feeling sorry for him--for anyone--was painful and Nancy liked to avoid pain. But something continued to draw her to the couple, like a safe she needed to crack. Why would he stay? How could he love a woman who was so cruel to him? Who thought he was with other women? She could understand his wife's worry. He was an attractive man, but even if he hadn't been, she'd probably make up a scenario to distrust him. But he was as straight as an arrow. No side life. Nancy followed him from home to work then back again. She didn't understand her fascination or how she would return the necklace, but it stayed with her. She thought of sending it back in an anonymous package. She thought about putting the necklace in his briefcase, but then realized that his wife would blame him for taking it and he wouldn't be able to explain it. But she knew she needed to do something to take the blame. She was ready for that.

* * *

Nancy went back to the house one evening and heard the raised voices. They were so loud this time she was certain the neighbors could hear. She could rob them blind and they wouldn't notice. She heard a baby crying, but that didn't let her stop her mission. It was a rush to be so close to getting caught, but she had to do it this way. She placed the necklace back where she'd taken it from, then moved something out of the way so that his wife would notice it. She turned to leave when she heard a scream.

Then a gunshot.

This time she couldn't stay in the shadows. She ran to the sound and saw the woman dead on the ground, a knife in her hand. The man stood over her, gun in hand, frozen. She was about to move to him when she saw a little figure unconscious on the ground, a pool of vomit nearby. Nancy raced over to the small form, and recognized the little girl. She turned her over and saw the large welt on the side of her head. She checked for a pulse and found a faint one. Nancy quickly put the pieces together. The mother must have struck the child and something must have snapped in him. He could take the blows, but he'd do whatever was necessary to protect his children, just as a mother would. But others wouldn't understand.

They'd see a big strong man and wouldn't grasp all that had lead to this one rash action.

"Drop the gun," she said.

He spun around startled. "What? What are you doing in my house?"

"Stealing."

"What?"

"You thought you were shooting at me. That's what you'll tell the police. Call them now."

"But--"

"Do you want your daughter to end up with no one?" she snapped, in no mood to argue.

"No."

"Then you're going to do exactly what I'm telling you. Call the police and tell them you confronted a burglar. You were protecting your home, your wife; I struggled, and she got in the way. That's the story."

He followed her instructions. Nancy ordered him to tie her up and she pulled out the necklace and had him make sure the police found it.

The police bought the story. She was booked for aggravated assault, home invasion and several robbery charges. She received a lengthy sentence, but she didn't care. She felt alive again. When she got out she'd do something different. She realized she'd grown tired of taking. Taking from other people's lives and living on their losses. This time she'd lost but had given instead. And it felt good.

Smoke Screen

Smoke Screen

Vanica Taylor was five-foot four and all attitude. She was someone I had never expected--or wanted--to see again. She arrived on my doorstep all five-foot six of her (she was wearing heels), false eyelashes, a bright pink shoulder-length weave and a cool attitude as if she expected me to drop down at her feet the moment I opened the door. I thought of closing it in her face. After dealing with high school students all day, I wasn't in the mood for another one. Especially the one who had skillfully and cleverly broken up my relationship with her father. She had been sly about it; even I had allowed myself to think that the cold, surly attitude was just a teenage shield that I would eventually be able to crack. I made it clear that I was in no way interested in being a stepmother, that I liked her father and left it at that.

She started her campaign against me early. It seemed like almost immediately, there were missed dinner dates, or interrupted ones. Tears and tantrums soon followed and her father doted on her, trying his best to please us both, and failing. I realized I didn't like her and that it was unfair for me to like him but think that his daughter was Satan's spawn. She really got under my skin and I soon discovered that it wasn't a 'teenager thing', it was her. She was razor smart, manipulative and scary. There was something dark and unsettling about her. To her delight, I broke up with her father. I thought I was just trying to beat him to the punch to be honest, the signs were so clear that the relationship was doomed I knew my days were numbered. Still, I think he was surprised when I said it wasn't working. At least he seemed so. I'm not going to pretend that I understand men well. Haven't had much practice. I had two really crappy relationships behind me but at forty-three I was hoping that I was getting the hang of things when I met Sidney and we did hit it off...except for Vanica.

So with that kind of history you can imagine that I nearly had a heart attack when she rang my doorbell. I wasn't happy to see her and she was clearly not happy to see me. She looked like she was suffering from indigestion or something.

I covered my surprise and pretended to be bored. "You lost or something?"

"I need to talk to you," she said, her tone matching mine.

"So far you're doing a great job."

She rolled her eyes making her disdain clear. "Can I come inside?"

I folded my arms. "No, what do you want?"

She sighed. "Look, I know I gave you a lot of shit before but I need to talk to you."

"About what?"

She rubbed her arms. "It's freezing out here."

She was right. It was early November and we were experiencing a brutal autumn. "If you're still smoking I'm sure you can warm yourself up."

Her upper lip curled. "I knew you were a bitch."

I smiled. She'd just given me the ammunition to do what I'd wanted to do. I closed the door.

The doorbell rang. Then I heard knocking.

"I'm sorry," she said. "Come on. It's important."

I swore. I wanted to walk away. I wanted to forget she was there. This was how she'd gotten me last time. One moment being a jerk and the next, pulling at my sympathy. I swore again--more at myself than at her--then opened the door. I yanked her inside then pushed her towards the kitchen.

She stumbled forward and swore. "No need to be violent," she said, absently smoothing down her coat sleeve where I'd grabbed her.

"Ready to call me a bitch again?" I pulled out a chair and sat. I wasn't going to offer her anything just in case she thought she could get comfortable.

"No, I'll just think it."

"Sit down and start talking, you have two minutes."

She sat down and smiled. "You really hate me, don't you?"

I leaned back and folded my arms. "You're not

improving my impression." I glanced at my watch."You're wasting time."

"I'm here because of my Dad."

I shook my head. "I'm not falling for that."

"It's true. My Dad is dating this other woman and she's awful."

I let my arms fall to my sides. "I don't believe this. You're here because your father is dating someone you don't like? What do you want me to do, help you find a way to break them up? And what's in it for me? Do you think I've been pinning away after your father all this time and would stoop so low to get back with him?"

"Would you?"

I stood. "Goodbye, Vanica."

She jumped to her feet. "That's not why I'm here. Well...it's only partially why. I do want you to help break them up but I have a good reason."

I gripped the back of my chair annoyed that I was curious."Why?"

"I think she's planning to kill my father."

I KNEW it was dangerous to believe her. Vanica loved her father and I didn't put it past her to come up with an outrageous story to get rid of another potential mother-figure. "What's your proof?"

"Twice Dad got real sick after she made dinner for him at her place."

"How sick?"

"He said it was a flu bug but I don't believe him."

"You think she poisoned him?"

"When she thought I wasn't looking she put some white powder in his drink. I threw it out. But I kept another one she made for him."

"Then go to the police."

"They won't believe me. I thought since you know a lot about chemicals, you could test it or something."

She was right. As a science teacher I knew a lot about ways to kill--I must admit that twice I'd thought of ways to get rid of her. No, I'm not proud of it, I'm just being honest. "Why would she want to kill your father when they aren't even married? What motive could she have?"

"She took out a life insurance policy on him."

That didn't sound good. And Sidney didn't seem the type of man who would be that blinded. Should I trust a girl who told me her father's favorite color was peach and then encouraged me to buy a dress, the same color--only to later let me find out that he hated that color because he was allergic to peaches? Then again, why would she come up with such an elaborate ruse? One that included an accomplice? She usually did her manipulations alone. Shortly after my breakup with Sidney I'd met another ex-girlfriend. Don't get the wrong impression, it wasn't like he had a string of women, she had only been number two, before me. Anyway, we shared our Vanica horror stories, but Vanica's devious actions had never involved anyone else. Why would this girlfriend be different?

Perhaps Vanica had met her match and wanted to use me to help her reach her end goal--to keep her father to herself. Poor Sidney, he'd waited years before even approaching the idea of going out on a date. Just getting babysitters, especially young ones, had been an ongoing nightmare, Vanica made sure none of them lasted more than one sitting, and Sidney waited to do some serious dating until she was old enough to stay home on her own, not wanting to go through all the trauma. Besides, the last incident, where Vanica locked herself in the bathroom and threatened to swallow a bottle of bathroom cleaning fluid if her dad did not come home right away, was the last straw. The babysitter had panicked and called 911 and the poison control center and a police officer arrived at the restaurant where he was with his date, to escort him back home to talk his daughter out of the bathroom.

"If you kept one of the drinks, with the white powder mixture you mentioned, you have enough evidence. You're very convincing. Or, if you want to get more proof, hire a private investigator. Whatever he or she finds out will give you enough material to go to the police."

"Why won't you help me?"

"Because I don't trust you."

Vanica blinked, then sniffed. "I thought you cared about my father."

I'd loved him really, but I'd never tell her that. I'd never tell her how painful it had been to tell him it wasn't working, to lie and say that it was me, but it was true. I couldn't love his daughter the way he wanted me to. I felt so, guilty wondering why other women could blend with their boyfriends' families, but I couldn't.

"You might as well get used to it," a friend of mine had

said. "At our age the men are going to come with baggage in the form of ex-wives, kids, or both."

"I'm sure there are some single guys without that," I said finishing off a plate of fried shrimp.

"Sure, but they're still living in their parent's basement or in a room over the garage."

"You're just cynical."

"All I'm saying is give it a little more time. I'm sure the kid isn't all that bad."

But she was. I lasted nine months. She won and I was out the door and now the little brat was here asking me to help her get rid of *another* woman thinking that she could use my feelings for her father to manipulate me. It had worked before but not this time. I yawned. "You gonna cry now?"

The approaching tears quickly dried up. "You don't believe me?"

"No."

"Why not?"

She seemed generally surprised so I decided to be honest. "Because you're smart. If you had evidence you'd go to the police and make them listen to you. You're not the type of person who would make allegations without proof."

She sighed. "Okay, you're right. I did go to the police."

"And?"

"And they said the powder was harmless. I even had a friend, who's mother works on the force, check Sherice's background and she said it's clean."

"So you have nothing to worry about."

She clasped her hands together until her knuckles were pale. "I don't like her."

"You don't like any of your father's girlfriends."

"No, I don't *trust* them. There's a difference. But with Sherice there's something I hate. Something I don't like. Like with you, it was different. I didn't like you and you didn't like me and it was cool, you know, because we knew where we stood, but with her...I mean. I knew that in the beginning you wanted to like me and you tried to like me, but you couldn't. But she's never tried. She didn't like me and she doesn't ever want to. She never tries to get to know me the way the others have."

"Maybe because she knows you'll never accept her. You know, you'll be off to college soon and your father may find someone who you don't get along with and--"

She pounded the table and raised her tone. "You're not listening to me."

I stopped. It wasn't like her to shout. Vanica was always cool and this outburst surprised me. Even when she threw a tantrum it was controlled, full of vitriolic words and tears. But this was an uncensored rush of emotion. There was one area where I saw the *real* girl behind the mask, when she talked about her father. Little did she know that our love for him gave us something in common.

"I'm listening," I said keeping my tone calm. "Tell me about her."

Vanica seemed uncertain. "You won't think I'm lying?"

"I told you I'm listening, it doesn't matter what I think right now. Tell me about her."

"She's cold, but she doesn't seem that way, you know? She looks so friendly and smiles a lot but it gives me chills each time."

"How long has she been seeing your father?"

"Four months."

"That's all and you think she has it in for him?"

"I told you about the life insurance."

"Why did your father consider it?"

"Because she said that *I* needed the security, just in case something happens to him. She said she's just making sure that I'll be okay."

I paused. "So the insurance is for you? Sherice's not on it?"

"No." I couldn't fully understand the problem. Sidney was a single dad and, while we didn't have time to discuss his personal finances, I was sure he already has some kind of life insurance for his daughter. He was responsible that way. Vanica must have misunderstood something. In discussion, his new girlfriend must have just suggested he increase the amount of coverage, there could be no other explanation. But I knew better than to introduce this line of reasoning into the equation.

"Then he's just looking out for you. Talking about death can be scary, but it's responsible for him to consider your future and--" Again I let my words drop away because I could see another shout coming. "Okay, okay. Keep talking."

"It's not about the money. She's making him act weird.

Dad's fallen for her hard. I know she's just a rebound after you, but I've never seen him like this. Before you, he'd at least listen to me, but now he won't. Now he says who he dates is none of my business."

"I'm sure he doesn't mean that. You're the center of his world."

"I used to be. Now it's Sherice. I'm really freaked."

"Do you need money to hire a private investigator?"

She shook her head. "No, I want you to talk to him. Since he won't listen to me, he may...what are you laughing about?"

I tried to stop laughing, really, but it was so funny. I eventually sobered and shook my head. "You really want me to look like a fool, don't you? How will I not look like some desperate ex who wants to break up a relationship that makes him happy? He'll cling to her even more. Come on Vanica. Get real, this is like Psych 101. If your father hated a guy you were dating you'd want to date the guy even more right, to prove a point?"

"Maybe."

"It will be the same with him."

"So you won't help me?"

I paused and studied her. "You're really scared?"

"Yea."

I didn't want to believe her, trust me. I had every reason not to. But I did want to make sure that Sidney was okay. It wasn't like him not to listen to Vanica, rebound relationship or not. Besides, I was used to making a fool of myself. I'd do it one more time. "So what do you want me to do?"

"I just want you to talk to my dad."

I didn't think it would make a difference, but promised I'd give it a try. I didn't know where I was headed.

* * *

I EXPECTED my reunion with Sidney to be awkward and I wasn't disappointed. Vanica orchestrated a meeting at the mall nearby where they lived. I passed by them as they were leaving a clothing store. I offered to treat the two of them to lunch, Sidney started to decline but Vanica spoke up about being hungry and he acquiesced, which didn't surprise us. He looked good. Annoyingly so. As delicious as my favorite Snickers bar. I almost wondered if Vanica had just wanted to show off how good-looking and happy her father was. I had almost wanted the fatalistic girlfriend story to be true. I had expected to see him with sunken eyes or shallow brown skin or gaunt features, but he looked the picture of health. Aside from the two incidents Vanica had spoken about I wouldn't have thought this man ever became ill.

We ordered food, found a table and Vanica started a stilted conversation then after a few minutes, put our plan into action. Vanica pulled out her cell phone, and said she had a friend she wanted to meet and that she'd meet us in the parking lot in thirty minutes. "If you see me first you don't know me," she said, then left.

"Vanica hasn't changed," I said wondering how I could get to the topic without sounding too nosy. *Hey*

Sidney, your daughter thinks your girlfriend is trying to kill you but how are things?

"Yes." Sidney replied. He adjusted his seat, looked around, awkwardly, then looked at me.

"You look good."

"You look great. Vanica told me how happy you are. I hear you're in a new relationship."

"You spoke to Vanica?"

"When you were getting your meal," I said quickly, to cover my blunder. "She wanted to rub my nose in how much better you are without me. And I'll be honest, I was a little jealous, but I'm glad you're happy." I sounded ridiculous because I'm not used to gushing or lying, but I was trying my best.

"I am. And you?"

"Still single. No surprise there."

His gaze became guarded and I don't know what I'd said wrong. He'd given me those looks before and I never knew why. I was never brave enough to ask, I liked ignoring problems and would always come up with a joke or something to make the look go away, but this time I had nothing to lose. "What did I say wrong?"

He looked surprised for a second then became still and I didn't think he'd reply then he sighed and said, "I hate when you do that."

"Do what?"

"Put yourself down. I know you think you're being funny but I hate it. I find it insulting."

"Insulting?"

"Yea. Say you liked butternut ice cream."

"I do."

"I know. Now imagine that I always make fun of butternut ice cream and say that anyone who likes butternut ice cream is stupid. How would you feel?"

"I'd hate it."

"Exactly. To me you're butternut ice cream. I like you and you go on as if liking you is stupid."

I didn't know what to say, I wish I did but I didn't. I wanted to say you really still like me? I like you too. But then I remembered we were no longer seeing each other and I still liked him too much to be friends. I was just here to make sure he was safe. "You're too nice a guy, you're supposed to hate me you know."

"Because you broke my heart?"

I nodded.

"I did, but then I met Sherice."

I didn't like the way he said her name and it wasn't because of jealousy this time. His face changed and I could see why Vanica was nervous. There was a strange wistfulness I'd never seen before that didn't seem right. It was as if another person had taken his place. "Tell me about her."

"Why?"

"Are you sure Vanica is your daughter? Don't you know anything about revenge? You're supposed to tell me how wonderful your new love is and how happy she makes you. So happy that you've almost forgotten about me."

He smiled. "Yes, you're right. What's your name again?"

"So, how did the two of you meet?"

He told me how they'd met but it wasn't remarkable. She'd approached him at a store and 'things just happened'--his words, not mine.

We talked and then his cell phone rang and he answered then swore. "Sorry hon' I'll be right there." He hung up and stood. "I have to go pick up Vanica. It's been over 30 minutes, I totally forgot we were to meet her."

"Just blame me, she'll enjoy that. Take care of yourself."

"Where are you parked?"

"I still have some more shopping to do."

For a brief moment, he looked as if he wanted to say more, but then stopped himself. "Okay, see you around."

* * *

I watched him leave. No warning signs from what he'd told me.

"Where are you?" Vanica asked me twenty minutes later when she called my phone.

"What?"

"You could have at least walked with my Dad to the parking lot."

"What for?"

"To get more information."

"I got plenty of information."

"Like what?"

"He's happy."

"That's because she's got him under a spell. Come

over tomorrow." She hung up.

* * *

THE NEXT DAY I went to their house and rang the doorbell. I had no choice. Vanica kept calling me until I promised I would come. Sidney answered the door, surprised to see me. He looked like he was ready for a date.

"I'm sorry Vanica invited me over," I said feeling my face burning.

Suddenly, she appeared. "There you are." She pulled me inside then escorted me into another room.

"What are you doing?" I asked.

"I want you to meet her. I've invited you over for dinner. She'll soon be here."

"Why didn't you tell me?"

"Because you wouldn't have come."

"Do you know how awkward this will be?"

"Yes."

"Well I'm not staying so that you can use me to ruin your father's date." At that moment I could barely contain my anger. She had lied, not the first time, just to get me to come over.

"But--"

I hurriedly left the room, anxious to be far away from Vanica, then I bumped into Sidney as he was coming around the corner. "I'm sorry about this. It won't happen again," I said in a rush. I opened the door then stared into the eyes of a woman who had no soul.

79

* * *

SHE HAD skin the color of mahogany and eyes as dark as Hades. I immediately knew why Vanica hated her. There was a darkness in her gaze that terrified me. She had that addictive attractiveness that only men see. I made my apologies to her then went to my car and slammed the door closed, as if I expected Sherice to be behind me. I fumbled for my phone and called Vanica.

"You were right," I said the moment she picked up.

There was a brief pause then a sound of relief. "So you believe me now?"

"I don't know what to believe," I said my heart still racing. "I'm not even sure what I saw."

"There's something wrong with her, but nobody else seems to think so."

"Don't worry. When she leaves, I'll follow her, to see if I can find out anything more."

That evening I waited, for several long hours in my car, for her to leave and followed her home. I didn't observe anything out of the ordinary. She stopped at the gas station, then at the local grocery store, before parking in her underground garage. I didn't find it necessary to try to enter her apartment building. Besides, I wasn't convinced I would be able to prove anything. That night I went home tired, and went to sleep wondering what I should do next, wondering if there was anything I could do about a feeling that I couldn't describe. I don't know how long I'd been sleeping before a sickeningly sweet smell woke me. I opened my eyes and saw Sherice standing in the corner. Even though the room was pitch dark I could see her clearly surrounded by a red glow. My skin felt as if it was on fire and I screamed. She covered her ears and grimaced. "Please don't do that."

"What are you doing in my room?" I pulled the blankets up close to for protection. I felt exposed. My skin suddenly felt cold.

"How much do you know?"

"What?" I asked, my voice hoarse from screaming.

"How much do you know?"

"I don't know what you're talking about."

"You recognized me."

I blinked, trying hard to adjust my gaze. I wasn't sure I was seeing what I was seeing. Was she scary and crazy too? "I don't even know you," I said wondering if there was a weapon close by to protect myself.

"Yes, you do. I could tell. Most of your type can't tell the difference, but you could."

"My type?"

She sighed sounding annoyed. "I really need my assignment to work so I hope you won't get in my way. I was called here. I have to do my duty."

"Called?"

"Yes, called, evoked, summoned doesn't matter. I'm supposed to be here. I don't want to have to hurt you, so please just stay away."

"What do you want Sidney for?"

"Who says I want Sidney?"

"Then who--?"

She pointed at me. "That's none of your business. Don't think too much, it will get you in trouble."

"Leave them alone."

She smiled--an ugly smile and the sickeningly sweet smell intensified. "Make me," she said then she was gone in a blast of red light.

Seconds later I had a strange sensation of waking up again as if the conversation had all been just a dream, even though I knew I had been awake. I briefly wondered if it had been my imagination or had she entered my dreams. I knew then that Vanica was right, Sherice was dangerous, but more than we knew. She could cast spells, but what Vanica didn't know was that Sidney wasn't her target.

* * *

"She's not human," I told Vanica the following evening at her house.

"What does she want?"

I paused, half surprised that Vanica hadn't argued with me. I wanted her to. I wanted her to tell me that I must be crazy saying that some strange alien woman wasn't after her father. Now I had to face the truth and deal with it. "I'm not sure," I lied not wanting to frighten her more than she was. "She says she's on a mission and that she was called here."

Vanica's eyes suddenly grew big. "What does that mean?"

"I have to confront her and find out," I said with a

growing conviction. I sat with Vanica in her living room, but felt uneasy.

Something was different about the house that I hadn't taken the time to notice before. You know how you can tell a lot about a place by the energy in it? Not just the items inside? Well, Sidney's spirit was no longer there. The air felt flat. The house he shared with Vanica used to have a warm, homey feeling, now it was just a building, like a sound stage with props not a proper home. Even when he greeted me moments after I'd arrived he seemed vibrant, but even that seemed to be just a veneer--a thin one. His smile was not quite his.

"Vanica and you friends?" he said, later that evening while Vanica finished preparing the meal and before Sherice arrived. "Amazing."

"A surprise to me too, but I'll take what I can get. I'm not the most lovable." I had slipped and put myself down again, but this time no wall came up. His gaze remained neutral. It didn't bother him, something that had, only a couple of days ago. "Are you feeling okay?"

"I'm feeling great. Better than ever."

He was happy, but there was a false ring to it, but I also knew he wasn't lying. Sherice arrived soon after and came into the living room, the sickeningly sweet smell preceding her. She walked over to Sidney and wrapped an arm around his waist. He leaned over and kissed her and I saw a brief wince cross her face as if the touch--or the affection--hurt, but it was gone quickly. Something pierced my chest, partly jealousy, because I knew then that I regretted letting him go, partly something else--fear.

She was stronger than I was, she knew something I didn't. And I didn't know how to find out what.

Vanica called us to dinner and we all ate and chatted, each morsel feeling like stones in my throat, but I swallowed them down. Then Sherice sent Sidney to the grocery store to get something--I still don't remember what--and the two of us were left alone with her.

She sat back and her voice changed. It became deeper, more melodic, reminding me of the dark red tinged vision that appeared in my bedroom. She sent me a hard look--but more with amusement than anger. "I told you to stay away."

Vanica spoke up. "I invited her."

She flashed an indulgent smiled at her. "You are greedy. You called us both here?"

"Called you?"

"Yes, evoked, summoned whatever you want to call it." She rested her hand on the table then began to drum her fingers, her brightly painted nails tapping a lazy beat. "Do you really think this mortal can beat me? Are you that selfish?"

"What are you talking about?"

She paused and lifted her hand from the table. "You're right. I'm through talking. I want to get this over with." She clasped her hands together, shifted her gaze to me and just stared. She did it so quickly I didn't have a chance to look away. At first I felt nothing then a sharp wave of pain. Suddenly, I was nine again and my father was shouting at me, verbal abuses that scared me with every word, ripping my soul to shreds; then I heard my first boyfriend telling me how ugly my body was, after we'd had sex, and telling me how no man would want me; then I heard Vanica's voice slyly telling me how many girlfriends her father had had and how I was one of many and that I wasn't even pretty. All these memories kept rolling through my mind and I fought them with my rage and felt my anger towards my father and my boyfriend and, even Vanica and then felt strong again and I met Sherice's cold dark eyes and I saw her smile and I almost smiled back.

Almost. But something stopped me, I'm not sure what. It may have been the way she smiled. At first it was encouraging and made me feel proud and then it became smug and triumphant and I wondered why my rage made her so happy. I shifted my gaze to Vanica. She looked horrified, terrified. Not for me but *of* me. She sat frozen in fear and for the first time I saw how young she was, that without the shield of her ugly attitude that she was just lost. She'd given me someone to hate and I'd taken the bait, but I didn't want to hate her now, although I felt the desire gnawing inside me. I saw a tinge of a red glow surrounding me.

I had to push back and love her anyway. But when I started to reach for her, an image of my father took her place. He sat where Vanica had been, and I yanked my hand back. I couldn't love him, I couldn't forgive his cruelty. Then I saw my first boyfriend and I drew back even more and I felt Sherice's sense of victory, because my heart was cold. I didn't have to forgive them or love them—just act as if nothing had happened. Hating them kept me safe and the red tinge glowed and part of it felt good because it made me feel powerful and protected. But I knew it was also burning me, singeing me, taking part of me, consuming me in both pleasure and pain.

I screamed and I saw Sherice cover her ears as she had in my bedroom and I continued to scream. I just screamed because I didn't want them--my first boyfriend, my father, even Vanica, anyone who'd hurt me-- still having power over me. I didn't want what they thought to still matter.

"No!" I screamed, closing my eyes. "You will not own me." Then I opened my eyes and I saw myself sitting there. But it was a different me. The me I couldn't stand to see. Myself with cold eyes, with anger, and I knew it was my shadow self who hated me more than anyone else could. And I stared back because I knew I could hate it more, if I needed to, in order to survive, but then the anger left my shadow self, and the image of me it left behind disgusted me.

All I saw were my weaknesses, the ones I hated most about myself. My desire to be loved, to be accepted, that made me vulnerable and I never wanted to be that vulnerable again. I looked at my weak self and recognized the challenge. Sherice was challenging me to accept this self and not hate it but love this self. Could I? Could I accept all her failings and faults, and not beat her down before anyone else could?

"She's pathetic isn't she?" Sherice said. "She's the reason your life sucks. It's okay to be ashamed of her. I would be."

I bit my lip not wanting to reply, tears burning my eyes.

"No one could possibly love that. She's stood in the way of all your happiness. You have no one else to blame but her. Your father was right. You're a loser."

Sherice said his words, imitating his voice, and I started to build up my rage to fight him, to fight her, to fight myself. Then I remembered that Vanica was frightened. I don't know why--or how--she penetrated my heart, but she did. All I kept thinking was, was she okay? Where was she? I had to get to her. I didn't care how my mind tried to delude me. I reached for where I knew she was. I reached for my despised shadow self. And then she became my father, but I still grabbed hold and he became my first boyfriend, but I didn't let go. "I love you," I said, my voice raw. "I love you." I said it unconditionally. I felt her grab hold of me and I held onto Vanica, not caring that she hadn't liked me, that she'd wanted her father to herself. I didn't need anything from her, I'd love her anyway. And the red tinge around me dissipated, the sweet smell diminished, replaced with a slight smell of smoke.

"I don't believe this," Sherice said. "Don't you remember what she did? You'll never be with her father."

I looked at Vanica. "I don't care."

I saw tears in her eyes and understood that Vanica's fear and rage had called this soulless entity into her life. That only I could save her from it. That it had tied itself to her long before I had come. Why I had sensed something dark about her, but now knew that I could free her. And I would. The fact that she'd reached out to me--why me? I didn't know, nor did I care. It meant she wanted something more than just her father's love, that her selfish love for him was destroying him and herself and she knew she needed help. "I love you," I said over and over, because it was something I'd never said before to anyone. "You are loved. Not just by your father, but by more if you let love in. The heart increases, only you make it shrink."

Sherice swore fiercely and shook her head. "I thought this assignment would have been easy. He was easy, the broken hearted ones are so eager to fill the void and Sidney was ripe to forget his pain after you left. He didn't want to feel anymore and I made sure that happened." She glared at Vanica. "I only made myself visible because she was ready and it was time. We could have been together for years. I could have given you so much-- money, independence, respect."

"It's time for you to go."

Sherice blinked lazily. "Are you sure Vanica?"

"Yes," Vanica added.

"You can't have him back, he doesn't want you," Sherice said to me.

"I don't care."

"You'll never have a real family."

I just stared at her. She shrugged. "Worth a shout.

You're stronger than I thought," she said then she disappeared in a blast of red smoke.

I woke up to see Vanica's tear stained face above me. I didn't even remember fainting.

"Are you okay?"

"She's gone."

"Good."

We heard the front door open and Sidney came into the hall carrying several grocery bags. He dropped them when he saw us. He rushed over. "What's wrong? What happened?"

"I fainted," I said sitting up. "But I'm okay now."

"Don't move. Do I need to call an ambulance?"

"No, really I'm fine." I just wanted to go home. I didn't want to be there when he asked about Sherice. I felt too fragile to deal with his disappointment. "I'm sorry to ruin your evening. I should go."

"Not before you tell me what you came here to say."

"What?"

"We're having a nice dinner and then all of a sudden you collapse."

"But what about Sherice?"

"Who?"

"Your girlfriend--" I stop when I see Vanica shake her head.

"You came over to talk to us," she said. "Dad went out to get something. There's no one else here but us."

I looked around the room and a sense of unhappiness was still there, just below the surface, but the house felt real again. He'd have no memory of the dark entity that had entered his home and nearly taken his daughter. I was glad for that. I looked at Sidney's eyes and they were wary but the expression didn't bother me. I welcomed his wariness. It meant he could feel pain and was shielding himself against it. I realized feeling pain was necessary. It was good to feel some pain. I wouldn't run from it or hide from it because its presence made joy that much sweeter. "I want a second chance with both of you."

He shook his head. "I don't know."

"I'm sorry. I didn't mean to hurt you."

"We'll see."

It was better than no and I was willing to take it. Trust had to be earned and I respected him for that. I knew that the memory of our breakup was still fresh in his mind. It would take time.

"Let's go get some sundaes," Vanica said.

"I just got back from--"

"Pleeaseeee."

"Okay."

"Good," I said. "I'll get strawberry."

"And I'll get Rocky Road," Vanica added. "What about you, Dad?"

"Butternut of course." He said, then grabbed his keys and opened the door.

Vanica and I shared a smiled and an understanding that would bind us for life, then walked towards a new future.

About the Author

Dara Benton is the pen name for Dara Girard, the award-winning, bestselling author of more than fifty novels such as *Honest Betrayal* and *Remember My Name*.

Visit her website to sign up for her newsletter and get sneak peeks, monthly updates on new releases, and special offers.

For more information visit
www.daragirard.com

ISBN (print): 978-1-958139-12-7
ISBN (eBook): 978-1-958139-11-0

Published by Riversong Books
An Imprint of Sulis International
Los Angeles | Dallas | London

www.sulisinternational.com

Other books by Markus McDowell
from Riversong Books

To and From Upon the Earth: A Novel

Onesimus: A Novel of Christianity in the Roman Empire

The Sky Over Chaos: Short Stories

Mortals As They Walk

For Elisa

Contents

There is nowhere so dark, so deep in shadow…

—Job 34.22

So Dense

He looked up from the journal he was reading as she shuffled into the room with her cane.

"Hey, Mom. I'm here in my chair."

"Oh! I didn't hear you come in. What are you doing home?" She went and sat in her chair with the ease of long practice. So effortlessly, a stranger might think she was sighted.

"It's Thursday."

"That's right," she said. "Your research and reading day. I lose track. What are you working on? Some fascinating new idea in nephrology?"

He sighed. "Mom. It's *nephology*. I study cloud formation and atmosphere, not the liver."

She cackled. "I know. And no one calls it nephology."

"True. So how long will you keep misnaming my field with a term that is no longer used?"

"Until I die. Just to keep you humble. Scientists always think their particular field is the most important of all."

"Well, you're not wrong," he said with a chuckle. What have you been doing?"

"Oh, just wandering to and fro upon the earth."

"You're so strange, mom. What does that even mean?"

"Exactly what it says."

"Sometimes I don't understand you." She laughed as her son shook his head.

She picked up one of her braille books and opened to a bookmark. "What are you working on, dear?"

"Nothing in particular at the moment. Just keeping up. A new article from a scientist at the Cern CLOUD facility, describing some of her work in the effects of the solar cycle and cosmic rays on cloud formation."

"Not research for your dissertation?"

"Not…directly. But I have to keep up in the field."

"More important to finish your doctorate."

"Good God, Mom, are you actually telling me to do my homework? I'm twenty-eight years old."

She smiled again. "But you still need your mom."

"True." He returned the smile. "I do."

Satisfied, she began sliding her finger over the book. They sat in silence for some time, until he finished the article and stood up. "Almost noon. Going to go check the weather."

He lay the journal on the table beside the chair and went through the dining room. As he slid open the glass doors to the balcony, he gasped.

"What is it?" his mom called. Her hearing was much better than most people. Among other things.

"Fog! Like I've never seen it!"

He ran back in to grab his tablet so he could read the data from his weather station mounted on the roof. As he sat down, he glanced at his mother. "What are you smiling about?" he asked.

She shrugged. "Nothing." *Blindess is such a gift.*

The car drove up the curving concrete ramp, tires squishing with a slight squeal. Reaching the roof of the parking garage, it headed to the opposite end. There was only one other the car in the entire lot, so the driver sped more than safety would warrant.

Across the way, high up in a hotel room, a man watched. He could barely see the car through the fog.

A woman sat in the other car, tapping on her phone.

Two birds sailed from high above, like tiny pterodactyls in the eerie light. They circled a tall apartment building, then swooped down to glide low across the shorter buildings, disappearing into the fog as they glided towards the bay.

A man got out of the car, now parked, and pulled his jacket close around him. As if on cue, the woman put her phone away and stepped out of her car. They both walked towards a stairway at the far corner.

"Hi, Penelope."

"Hello, Juan. I was just enjoying the fog."

He motioned her ahead of him at the stairs. "Yes, thicker than normal at this time of year."

"True. Although it's also been colder this time of year."

"By the way, did you see the new job numbers?"

"I did. A disaster. This administration has no idea what they are doing."

"Oh, I don't know. They are still trying to stop the decline from the last administration's policies."

"It's been a year, and it's gotten worse. We'll see."

The captain of the fishing boat muttered as he examined the screens above the helm.

"What is it, Skipper?"

He frowned. "Haven't seen fog this thick for a long time in this harbor. Might should've layed off a bit."

The First Mate peered out the window. "I still can't see the docks. How close are we?"

"Less than a quarter of a mile."

"I can't even see any of the big buildings."

The captain looked up and peered into the white expanse. "I think I can see the top of some building right there."

"Don't think so…" The First Mate stared where the Captain was pointing. "That just looks like a darker bank of fog. See how it curves on the right?"

"Maybe." He looked back down at the instruments. "I can tell by the depth and the radar where we are, but if this was an unfamiliar port, I wouldn't risk it. Hey, did you get someone to take a look at the davit?"

His shipmate frowned. "You told me you had already called someone to meet us there."

"No, I didn't. I told you to make sure you called someone to meet us there."

An award silence ensued. "Sorry, Skipper, I guess I misunderstood." His tone said otherwise, but his words respected the chain-of-command. "I'll go call now." He fished his phone out of his pocket and headed aft.

The woman stood at the waterfront walkway, staring out into the bay. Not that she could see anything. To the left, the sea faded into a white-gray nothingness about 100 feet away. As if someone had airbrushed the world out of existence.

It felt as if the air was packed in cotton. "Fitting," she said aloud. The word was enveloped and disappeared. She smiled grimly. *Like dad.* One week, he was here: alive, working around the house, telling his funny stories, and then—

She wanted to avoid reliving that event, but it came flowing back. Finding him collapsed in the garage. The paramedics. He squeezed her hand before they lifted the gurney. Her long, fearful drive to the hospital. And that was it. Forever.

She had *told* him he needed help. Repeatedly, until he yelled, "Let me be!" He had never spoken to her like that. Not since…not since she asked him about mom, and all the horrible things she had said about him. Back then, he apologized for his harsh words and explained how difficult it was to hear those same lies repeated by his ex-wife. Someday, he told his daughter, he'd tell her the truth about what her mom had done.

Now she would never learn the truth.

At least she got to talk to him before he slipped into a coma. Like the sea before her, he faded away until he was gone. Merciful, perhaps, considering the damage to his heart. But now it was her heart that was damaged.

Her tears mixed with the droplets in the fog, becoming one with the ecosystem.

"Okay. See you Saturday." He stepped out the back door and stopped. "Wow!"

"What is it?" his boss said from back inside the restaurant.

"Foggy. Never seen it this thick! Crazy.

Suzanne appeared at his side. "Yeah. Can't even see our cars."

It was like the world ended three feet in front of them. He looked up. Just a whitish-gray expanse. "It's so quiet."

"You okay driving home?"

"What choice do I have?" He shrugged. "If it's too much, I'll just walk. It's only about a mile and half."

"You could stay here."

"At the restaurant? No, thanks." He rolled his eyes.

He looked at her as she stared out into the fog, a funny expression on her face.

"What is it, boss?"

"Nothing. I need to get back and finish the bank." She turned away. "Don't forget to shut the door." She went back in, shaking her head. He was either an idiot, or she was not as interesting as she hoped.

He stood, watching her walk back down the service hall. Funny how the fog was only out here, but not inside. He could see her clearly, sixty feet away, until she turned into the office at the far end. Turning back, it was like entering a white cotton candy world.

The data from his sensors on the roof were confusing. It was unusual to have arcus formations this far from the coast, at least without major storm activity. In fact, the formations almost look like roll clouds. That was something he'd never seen here. He tapped over to the chat forum on his tablet, and let out a "harumph" as he read.

"Is the weather showing some unusual patterns?" It was his mom, standing in the doorway. He was often amazed at how a blind woman could be so stealthy.

Still reading, he said, "Yes. Quite."

After a few seconds, he looked up from the tablet and over at her. "How did you know that?"

"I can just tell."

"How?"

Her smile dropped. "Uh, well, by the sounds you make, I guess."

"That makes no sense. Anyway, people are reporting St. Elmo's fire in some of the higher elevations. In the fog!"

"And that's unusual?" she asked, still smiling like the Cheshire Cat.

"Yes, of course it is. They are probably wrong—dense fog plays with people's eyesight because they are not used to being blind."

"No, they aren't, are they?" She gave a short laugh. But he was no longer paying attention to her.

The radio crackled. Jeremy stopped talking. He and Chas waited for the voice.

"Car 37, do you copy?"

Jeremy tapped the button. "Car 37 here, we copy. Over."

"Affirmative, 37, we have a multiple car incident on Highway 40 at mile marker 115. Proceed immediately. Ambulances in route. Over.

"Copy that, dispatch. On our way. Over and out." He clicked off the radio.

Chas reached up and flipped on the siren, checked the mirrors, and began to perform a U-turn. "Watch for me."

Visibility did not extend more than ten feet in any direction. Chas made the turn and proceeded at less than ten miles per hour. Both officers peered to the front and each side of the car, watching for any landmarks or lights—and especially for people.

Jeremy tapped on the screen, frowning. "There is no mile marker 115 on Highway 40."

"Call it in."

Jeremy already had the mic. "Dispatch, confirm mile marker on Highway 40."

"That's 115, Car 37."

"No mile marker 115 on the map. Say again."

Silence for a few seconds, then the radio crackled to life again, but calling another unit to a different location. Another traffic accident.

Then another. And another. And a third.

"Car 37? One hundred fifteen is what we have. I see it on my map. Head to highway and I will confirm momentarily."

Jeremy shook his head. "Who is that?"

"Sounds like Jenny. She knows her stuff."

"Well, mile markers only go to 67 in the county."

"She'll sort it out."

"Okay. Gonna be a bad night. Never seen it like this."

"Yeah. Eyes sharp. Let's not be one of the accidents."

"God, I can't see anything up the trail."

"Neither can I. If you get more than ten feet in front of me, you disappear. It's kind of freaking me out." She took a swig from her water bottle, panting a little at the exertion from their uphill climb.

Kimmie looked at her. "It's just fog." She was not even slightly winded.

Kathy worked out more than Kimmie—cardio and strength—yet these weekly hikes always seemed more difficult for her than Kimmie. It sometimes made her mad.

"Because it is so quiet and still, and feels like I've gone white blind." She pulled out an energy bar. "Want half?"

Kimmie looked around. "I'm fine." She peered up the trail in the direction they were heading. "I think we're close to that ledge. Stay on the right, though it's almost impossible to see landmarks. But my tracker says we've come almost 2 miles."

"Should we go back? I mean, that ledge—"

"Nah, it's fine. Just stay to the right."

Kathy found her irritating when she did this. If Kimmie wasn't concerned, then no one should be either. She had so little compassion or insight.

Yet she'd always been that way. They'd known each other since college, and Kimmie had always been a good, steady friend. But not one you'd turn to for sympathy or feelings. "Okay. Let's go."

Kimmie turned and trudged up ahead, her sturdy legs hitting a steady rhythm, the crunch of her boots on the trail—the only sound in this dense fog other than Kathy's panting.

Kathy slipped her bottle back into her rucksack while trying to keep up. Despite Kimmie's words, it was scary not being able to see her if she got too far ahead on the trail.

The dirt path was fairly level, but soon turned up and to the left. Kathy remembered this section. Kimmie was right, the ledge was coming up. It was a drop-off on the left, with a cliff edge on the right. The trail was pretty wide, and not a problem when visibility was good. But it made her anxious knowing that there would be a chasm to the left.

Kathy's breathing was labored. She was heavier than Kimmie—not fat or overweight, just "big-boned," as her mother used to tell her. That's probably why she had less stamina. More weight to lug up the hill.

She didn't want to ask for another rest stop so soon. Looking up, Kimmie was no longer visible. *Keep going*, she said to herself. *One foot in front. Stay to the right edge of the trail. Wait for the cliff to appear.*

She heard a sound and jerked to a stop.

"Kimmie? Was that you?"

Nothing.

"Kimmie? Are you there?"

"Kimmie!"

The data was becoming even more unusual. He left his tablet for his computer, accessing the lab instruments at the university. The density levels from all the sensors, even the ones out in the suburbs, was historic. At least as far as he knew. This was going to take some work. He needed to get into the research databases, but he didn't want to stop watching the incoming sensor data and monitoring the chat room.

It made no sense, because the prevailing wisdom among scientists—for many years now—was that the increases in global temperatures were causing the reduction in cloud covers that had been going on for decades. And— "Wait!" he said to himself, and switched over to the solar data. Low solar activity had been posited to cause an increase in the cloud cover of the planet, cooling it down. Doesn't really explain the sudden onset of this history-making fog, but if there had been no activity for some time…In fact, the last two weeks showed *increased* solar activity. Ah well, the effect of solar activity was just a theory.

He picked up his phone and tapped a name.

"Hey, James. You watching this?"

"Of course. I really don't know what to make of it."

"I was just looking at solar activity, to see if—"

"—no, it's up, and also, it's not statistically proven—"

"I know, I know. Was just calling to see if you had any other theories. Or maybe I just wanted to talk to a colleague because this isn't just a scientific curiosity."

"You're not wrong. I've been watching the news. Some are saying it's not natural."

"Human created? How?"

"Don't know. Right now, it's just a few people suggesting it, and a lot of amateurs on the feeds."

"That seems crazy. And why?"

"Environmental terrorism."

"*Environmental terrorism?* Come on. To what end? A bunch of car crashes and having to stay inside?"

"Hey, you asked. I'm just telling you what I hear."

"Well, that's just idiotic and could cause unnecessary panic. What are they thinking? The density levels are still growing and should really already have stopped at this dew point with the temperature settling in after sundown."

"I'll let you know if I heard anything worthwhile."

"Thanks. Same here."

He disconnected and sighed. "Environmental terrorism," he said.

In the other room, his mother laughed quietly. "Indeed. Ridiculous," she whispered to herself.

"Siri, turn on the television to local news." She smiled as the technology assistant responded and the news came to life. Yes, she was old and blind, and did not understand the technology, but she appreciated her son setting it up for her.

"—unprecedented in history, the experts are telling us. We're going to go back to our correspondant at the harbor, Anna, as soon as we can re-establish the connection. We don't think the fog had anything to do with it, but our techs are still working. Let's...let's go to Susan, who is in downtown near the government center. Susan?"

"Thank you, Robert. We are getting reports of traffic accidents all over the city. Authorities urge everyone to stay indoors, no matter what. First responders need the roads clear. We also have reports of power outages, fires, and a building collapse. We're still gathering information, but please stay where you are. The fog is not expected to lift until late tomorrow morning."

"Thanks, Susan, for that important message. We've all probably driven in fog, but we've never seen anything like this. Please be safe out there...we've...we've just never seen anything like this...it looks like we have Anna back, so let's go to her by the Fifth Street pier—"

"Siri, turn off the television." The silence returned.

She chuckled and closed her eyes, seeing everything she needed to see.

So Humane

The cell was dark and damp; the dirt floor covered with dried rushes. They were not fresh. No bench, no chair, no low stone bed.

The man sat huddled in one corner. He had pulled together some rushes to make an ersatz cushion. Still, the cold emanating from the nearby walls seeped through his thin garment. At least it was warmer now that it was in April—the winters were cold here in the center of Paris.

His excrement was piled in the far corner of the cell, a psychological attempt to remove himself from the stench. The guards tossed a bucket into his cell every few days, to collect the defecation with his hands. He was not able to wash except when they delivered his food once a day: a hunk of cheese, a thick slice of bread, and a bowl of water. Since he also needed the water to drink, his washing was miserly. The meager attempts at hygiene and health had little effect on the piss-and-shit smell of the cell. He was filthy, even after the ablutions, but the ritual made him feel like he had some control over this miserable life.

There was a small opening in the heavy wooden door to the cell, reinforced with iron. It was just large enough for a guard to peer through or pass the board through. They had to open the door to retrieve and return the bucket. A faint, indirect light came through the cracks around the door—presumably from the torches that lined the hallway. He had only seen that hallway once, seven weeks ago when he had been brought in. At least he thought it was seven weeks. From the first day, he made little scratches at feeding time on the floor in one corner. He assumed they corresponded to days, though there were no cycles of light and dark to know for sure.

To an outside observer, it would appear that he was curled up in the corner, hugging his knees, staring out into the cell, unmoving. Every few moments his head moved slightly. This outside observer might assume that he had lost his mind, or was in a stupor from the beatings and the conditions. Perhaps reflecting on his crimes. Or wondering what would come of him to him.

In fact, he was engaged in a mental exercise concerning the stones of the cell, which were rough rectangular shapes. They were a dirty white-gray, but without more light he could not be sure. The first row of blocks were laid end to end. The mortar had been slopped between them when the prison was built. Some of it was crumbling, but the stones were so close together, and so large, there was no chance of digging one out. Besides, even if he did, there would be so many more obstacles beyond this cell that it would be a futile effort.

The next row of blocks were laid on top of the others, but staggered so that each block was sitting half on one below, half on the next one below. The result was that no mortar line ran straight up the wall, adding stability. The third row was back in line with the first row, and this alternating pattern continued to the ceiling, which was made of thick wood beams, with more stones laid on top. Another cell, he assumed.

His mental exercise consisted of counting those blocks. He began at the wall opposite the door, and counted across, moving up at the end of each row. On the alternating rows, where the builders began with a half-block, he counted one half. Once finished with one wall, he began on the wall to its left, then on the wall to its right. To count the blocks of the wall in which the door was set, he had to crawl to the center of the cell and look back.

At first, he stood in the center of the cell to count, but he was so weak these days he sat. He wasn't sure if he was sick, or if the paucity of diet made him feeble.

He had performed this exercise many times. Sometimes he lost count, and he then forced himself to start over. Sometimes he came up with different numbers, off by one or two from a previous counting. Usually, there were three hundred and twenty-one and a half, so he was pretty sure that was the correct number. It was a mind-numbing exercise that took him out of his environment, out of his condition, and into a world dominated by the order and mental focus.

He was in the midst of counting when a noise at the door startled him. He heard keys in the lock, and the door swung open.

"Prisoner! To the far wall!"

He knew the routine. It was the same every time they brought the shit bucket. But it had only been one day. Had he lost count?

He rose and hobbled to the far wall and turned to face the door, as he had been taught. The door opened the rest of the way, and he saw two guards—not the usual single guard with the bucket. The livery and the gilded sword of the second man betrayed an officer of some importance, not a common jailer. As if to punctuate that fact, the man's face cringed at the stench. "Merde!" he said with a turn of his head.

He turned back to the prisoner and spoke. "Nicolas Pelletier! I am Antoine Brissot, the official representative of Charles-Henri Sanson, the High Executioner of France. I am here to inform you of your sentence," he said, chin raised. "For the crimes of highway thievery which you have committed, tomorrow morning at nine o'clock you will be put to death."

The words were no surprise. He knew his fate soon after his arrest and brief trial. Highway robbery was a serious crime in France, more so than common thievery, for it preyed on the wealthy as they traveled in their fancy stagecoaches. The knowledge of his pending death, even when expected, seemed unreal.

He had seen death, of course. He had known people who existed and then did not. Sometimes he was the cause of the demise. But he could not fathom his own nonexistence. Should he scream? Protest? Fall on the floor and beg for mercy? He felt nothing.

"I am also to inform you," began Brissot, as a bit of sardonic glee crept into his tone, "that the Assemblée Nationale has recently decided that the purpose of the death penalty is not to make a sinner suffer, but to remove him from society. Therefore, you will not be hung, beheaded, or dismembered. No, a new age dawns in France, the beacon of the world. We will be humane."

Nicolas looked up. A reprieve?

"I see you are surprised. But even a common thief like you knows that France is the epitome of advanced culture and the pinnacle of society throughout all of history!" He paused, raising his chin in the air. "You will be the first prisoner to be executed using a new device. It is called the *louisette*. The people are ecstatic to see this new device in action. So your infamy continues, right up to the moment of your death and beyond!" He paused for dramatic effect, which seemed childish to Nicolas. "In fact, I believe this new device was invented by an Alsacian. You hail from Strasbourg, is it so?"

His mind reeled with all this information. No reprieve, but a new *device*? "louisette" was a personal name, giving no clues to the nature of the device. Probably named after the inventor or the king.

Nicolas nodded.

"I thought so. A Monsieur Laquiante is the inventor. You might know him, since he is an officer of the court in Strasbourg." He smiled.

"No," Nicolas replied, "most of my best work was around Île-de-France." It felt good to be flippant, though he did not know why.

The liveried officer looked at him for a moment, as if considering whether Nicolas' response was disrespectful. "Your 'work.'" The officer waved dismissively. "Eh, bien." He nodded to the guard, and with a flourish and a slam of the door, they were gone.

The cell was dark and damp. The prisoner was curled up in a corner, staring at the opposite wall. He was in the midst of his regular mental exercise when keys jangled at the door. The door swung open and slammed against the wall. In came Brissot and two soldiers.

"Prisoner! On your feet!"

He blinked. This was different.

He struggled to his feet with a hand on one wall to steady himself, it dawned on him that he had not been ordered to the far wall. One of the soldiers walked behind him; the other strode to the middle of the cell in front. Now he could see more soldiers standing at attention outside the cell. Their muskets were in the ready position.

This was it.

"Follow me!" Brissot shouted—unnecessarily loud, it seemed to Nicolas. As Nicolas followed, the two soldiers fell in behind. The rest—maybe four or five gendarmes—took places in front and behind. As they marched, his mind wheeled. Moments of sheer panic interspersed with analysis and thoughts that seemed a contrast to the doom that lay ahead. As they moved through the darkened corridor, Nicolas began counting the doors along both sides. He wondered about the prisoners in those cells. What fate were they awaiting? He knew that the Prison de la Grand Roquette housed both those to be executed and those awaiting less harsh punishments.

What was this new device, this *louisette*? Nicolas did not fear death. When he spurred his horse and descended upon an unsuspecting carriage, he knew that the coach driver might have a musket and could get off a shot before Nicolas. What if one of the passengers was a soldier? Unlikely perhaps, but still a risk. Sometimes, when he visited Paris, cloaked and hooded, he feared recognition by a former victim and a call to authorities. Again, unlikely. Back then, it caused him anxiety. He did not want to die.

Waiting for his execution in prison had cured him of that particular fear. He would face death with apathy. Hanging? It was usually over as soon as the noose tightened and broke the neck. Even if there was no break, strangulation came within minutes. Nothing to fear. But he *had* seen men tortured to death because of certain crimes. Dismemberment was common, and he had heard pathetic victims howl like an animal as the executioner held up his severed limbs. Disembowelment was even more gruesome—the prisoner watched as the hooded butcher pulled out bloody entrails. The indescribable smell. The crowd yelling and cheering as a modern equivalent to Roman gladiator shows.

But this new thing, this *louisette*—what did it mean? Was it a torture? Or just some new method of hanging?

The hallway curved and they arrived at a crosswise hallway, though not at a precise ninety-degree angle. It was larger and better lit. He blinked. His eyes had not been exposed to this much light in many weeks. Far down the hall was an even a brighter light, up high. A window?

What if Bissot was playing with him? A new invention for punishing the "worst of criminals"? Nicolas had heard nothing of this. But he knew how executions worked. The people gathered to cheer someone else's pain. "There is a person far worse than me…" We hate most what we fear in ourselves. "Am I capable of doing what he did?" The thought terrifies us, so we must kill it, wipe it out, so it can no longer remind us of our own flaws. Much safer than trying to understand it.

The company of men slowed and stopped near the opening, now high above. His eyes continued to adjust. Two massive wooden doors in front, crossed and beamed with iron. He could hear a faint buzzing sound from beyond it.

Bissot and a guard exchanged a few words. Two soldiers moved to the side of the doors, struggling with weighty chains and bolts. The clanking of heavy chains and locks echoed down the stone corridor behind them. The noise stopped, and each guard grabbed a door handle, leaned into them, and pushed with their weight. The doors began to open.

A vertical sliver of illumination appeared from the floor up to the top of the door frame. It grew wider, as did the brightness, as if a rip in the universe was opening to the throne room of God. The buzzing he heard was the noise of a crowd talking and murmuring beyond the doors.

Soon the light was so intense that it hurt. The guards began to move forward, but he could not make out anything in the bright light. A shove from behind made him stumble to his knees, as if he was falling in mercy before the Shekinah.

"On your feet, prisoner!" He was seized by both arms and hoisted to his feet. For a moment, the aroma of soap touched his nostrils. Bodies nearby that had been washed with clean water. It was the closest to a human he had been in some time, and he became painfully aware of his own stench. Since he had been tossed into his cell, no one had touched him. He felt a sensation of intimacy—strange since these were the same guards leading him to his death. Even the touch of an enemy is better than no touch at all.

He shuffled forward, now without the help of the guards, through the doorway. His eyes began to adjust. The day was not bright after all, but overcast and gray. The public square before him was an undulating mass of people. The close-packed buildings, of various sizes and ages, lined the square. Streets ran off in different directions out of the square. Something large stood between him and the crowd. A fountain? A statue?

He was led towards the structure, and as he drew close, he saw that it was not a monument at all, but a tall, wooden frame, with metal reinforcements and a base, sitting on a plinth of stone.

"Step up," said a quiet voice to his right. Below the plinth was a short flight of stairs, just wide enough for three to walk abreast. He climbed the steps with one of the guards and was brought to stand before the contraption, three times as high as a man. Two men stood beside the structure.

Nicolas' brow furrowed as he looked at the bottom of the frame. There was a thick board, set on edge, running from one side to the other; the top about two feet off the ground. In its middle was a half-circle cutout. It reminded him of public stocks. The wrongdoer places his neck on the half-circle and the wrists in the small half-circles to either side. The guards slide the other board on top and lock it in place. The prisoner is fixed in place with his head and hands caught between the two boards. The criminal was on public display, like a trapped animal, where the righteous masses could ridicule the ugly beast, spit upon him, and use his head for target practice with rotten fruit and garbage.

But the stocks were not a new invention, nor were they for executions. The presence of metal brackets on either side of the vertical struts made sense of stocks, but the lack of smaller half-circles for the wrists did not. A second board, leaning against the side of the structure, with a similar single half-circle cut, matched up to the bottom board—but again, no wrist cutouts.

Were they going to lock him in there and then dismember him? That wasn't efficient, and the contraption would block the public's view. Usually they merely strapped the criminal to a table before beginning the cutting.

He raised his eyes. Why was it so tall?

Realization crept over him like a dark, cold mist. At the top of the structure, suspended by a rope between the two struts, was a large, heavy iron blade, the bottom edge honed to shiny sharpness. The edge was curved down in the middle. The rope passed through a series of pulleys to the side, slanting down to the edge of the platform, where the end was lashed to a metal cleat, like a boat of death moored to a dock. An oaf of a man, dressed in black with a hood over his eyes with only his mouth and chin visible, stood beside the cleat.

He rocked back and forth as if he could not wait to cast off the grisly vessel on its maiden voyage.

The crowd roared. Nicolas became aware that Bissot had been standing at the front of the platform speaking. He gazed out over the people, a blur of humans packed together, spreading out like a strange carpet of hair, hats, hoods, and bonnets, filling the space all the way to the buildings and down the adjoining streets as far as he could see. More people lived in the Eleventh Arrondissment than any other section in Paris—the most densely populated area in *any* city of Europe—and it appeared they had all turned out to watch Nicolas and his appointment with the louisette.

Nicolas was terrified. How did this work? Was he to place one arm in the cutout to have it chopped off by the lowered blade? Then the other? Then his legs? Was it merely a new way to dismember him before he bled to death? Would the oaf lower the heavy blade slowly? Perhaps up and down, make a deeper cut each time. Was it—

Wait. Slow down. Bissot said it was more "humane." He wasn't quite sure what that meant. But at minimum, it would not be torture, correct? He could relax.

The unknown was making that difficult.

Bissot had stopped speaking and the crowd was yelling and screaming. Hands grabbed his arms from either side to force him forward. This time, Nicolas felt no intimacy.

"To your knees." He knelt before the device and began to sweat and shake. Fear and panic were his masters now, despite his previous resolve to meet his death with studied stoicism and the single word he held on to: "humane." He intended that his last act of defiance would be to rob the bastards of any pleasure in his death. But he thought he'd be hanged by the neck until dead—a shock and brief struggle, then over. Or perhaps a few moments of strangling, but he could handle that. This unknown device was making his mind betray him.

A guard forced his head down and his neck into the shallow cut. He began to struggle against his own volition as the top board was placed over his neck and latched. Trapped! When would the blade come down? The crowd was roaring. He fought with himself not to cry out, tried to calm his mind. Humane! This was humane! He pulled and pushed against the boards. He was a madman. A moan and a grunt escaped his mouth.

The crowd went silent. A reprieve? He stopped struggling. Humane. Everything was okay. He tried to take a breath.

"Commencez!" a voice shouted. Individual screams and jeers from the crowd sounded out, with more joining in the hue second by second. Another cry erupted unbidden from his throat. His body, on its own again, struggled against the boards. He defecated. The crowd noise swelled. A wooden and metallic clunk sounded from above. Like a stagecoach being unhitched. Metal scraped on wood.

Nicolas screamed.

So Kind

"He was so kind." She smiled, almost embarrassed.

Ashley smiled back. "What do you mean? He didn't ask you to pay your half like the last guy?"

Darla laughed. "Ugh. That was a disaster. It wasn't so much that he wanted to split the meal. It was our first date, and it wasn't like he had formally asked me out. But he wanted to split it when he'd ordered twice as much as I did. Then he got me a *cab* home while he drove off in his car."

"Oh yes," Ashley laughed. "I forgot about that. Such losers out there."

"Yes. And I hate this online dating, but this time—"

"Look, a lot of people find 'the one' on those sites. I told you about Kami—"

"Yes, yes, I know. I've done it four times—five now—and every one turned out to be nothing like their picture or their profile. Until now."

"So how is this guy different?"

Darla shrugged. "He seemed...*normal*. No showing off. No pretentiousness. He was polite and took care of me without seeming needy or creepy."

"In what way?"

"Like, he opened doors for me, but didn't run ahead to do it like he was trying to impress me. It wasn't an act. He touched my arm a few times as we talked, but it always seemed natural and unassuming."

"Okay…"

"And he didn't talk about himself incessantly like the others. Remember that first guy? 'Oh, I've made so much money this year.' 'Do you know the singer Paul Simon? I've met him.' 'Lots of women want to go out with me, but most are just after my money.' I wanted to throw up."

Ashley laughed. "Yes, so desperate to impress, but only talk about things that would impress guys, not women."

"Right?" She leaned forward. "I guess that's what I'm saying. This guy was just …relaxed. Hate to use the word, but he was genuine."

"Okay." She pursed her lips. "But it's only one date. What's next?"

"He invited me over for dinner. Wants to cook for me. Says he loves cooking—his mom was a chef."

"To his apartment?"

"House. He owns a house."

"You know why he's inviting you over."

She shook her head. "I don't think so. He said if it was too soon, we could just go to dinner or a movie or a club again. He'd like to cook for me someday, if we continue to hit it off, but no hurry. He even told me not to answer right away, but tell him later."

"Hm."

"What?"

Ashley shrugged. "I don't know. Perhaps I've been married too long. But when something sounds too good to be true…it usually is."

"Maybe. I'm reserving judgment. Been through too much. But so far, so good."

Ashley waved at the waiter to bring the check. "So you told him you'd come?"

"Not yet, I wanted to see what you thought."

Ashley took the device from the waiter, put in a credit card, and handed it back. As Darla protested, she held up a hand. "This is my treat. I've been far too busy lately, and it is so good to see you." She looked into her friend's eyes. "If you feel good about it, then tell him yes. If he has a house, he's got stability. You say he seems natural and unassuming. And he wasn't pushy about it."

"Not at all. In fact, before he dropped me off, he said not to worry about it, he'd call me later in the week and we'd go out a few more times if I was uncomfortable with coming over on the second date."

She smiled. "But you are already comfortable."

Nodding, Darla said, "Yes. I really am. Surprisingly."

"Then do it. You deserve a nice guy."

"Thank you, Ashley."

His house was immaculate. Not super fancy, but it was clear he liked nice things. It was sparse, as if he saved up money to buy quality things one at a time, rather than decorating and stocking with make-do items.

The decor was also unassuming. As if he did it because *he* liked it, not to impress guests. When she remarked on a painting hanging beside the television, he almost seemed embarrassed.

"I…it was more than I wanted to spend. I had been saving for it, but not sure I should spend the money. Then I got an unexpected bonus at work. My best friend told me I should use the money and get it. It would make me happy."

She smiled. "And does it?"

"It does. But also a bit guilty."

He led her into the kitchen where he had pots and skillets popping and simmering. "I hope you like fish. This is a salmon fillet, with a special seasoning my mom made up."

"Sounds wonderful." The kitchen was well appointed, not surprising if he inherited a love of cuisine from his mother. In fact, it looked as if he'd spent more money in here than the rest of the house.

He expertly flipped the two fillets over and cut slightly into one, "Just about ready."

She watched as he moved smoothly around the kitchen, handling the utensils and cooking implements with the ease of experience. He cut up vegetables with that rapid tap tap tap of skilled chefs. He welded knives like they were extensions of himself, and she could see he kept them razor sharp. Seasonings were applied with his fingers out of little bowls, washing his hands before and after. As he plated the fish, vegetables, and sauces, she noted the attention to detail and presentation. He was telling the truth about cooking.

She was impressed.

Finally, he finished and stepped back. "Okay." He sighed. "Perhaps not my best effort—I'm a little nervous. Been a while since I cooked for anyone. Anyone like you, anyway."

She dimpled. "If it tastes anywhere close to how it smells, it will be fantastic."

He cocked his head and smiled back at her. "You're too sweet." He turned back and, from a drawer, handed her eating utensils. "Do you mind?" He said, nodding at the dining table.

"Of course, chef."

"Ha, no." He took the plates up and followed her. "That was my mother. I'm a pale imitation."

The dinner was exquisite. He really had learned well from his mother. They talked—about their respective work, about the Panthers terrible season, about the movies they enjoyed, and go-to cocktails. They had a lot in common. For over two hours they sipped wine, nibbled on cold remnants, and shared their stories. She felt herself warming to him in a heartfelt, comfortable manner that she had not known in many, many years. It was like her heart was coming out of hibernation.

After she helped him clear the table, he said it had been a wonderful night. "You are special," he said, "and I'd love to spend more time. Maybe watch a movie or something? But if you need to leave, that's okay, too, and I'll just look forward to the next time."

"Oh, I'm not ready to go yet," she said, perhaps with a bit more enthusiasm than was proper at this point. "I mean, if that's okay." Too bold?

"No, I was hoping you'd say that. Let's watch something."

He smiled, took her hand, and led her into the living room. It was warm and inviting. He sat on the couch first, silently allowing her to choose where to sit and how close.

She sat close up beside him, feeling the warmth of his body against her.

He picked up the remote. "Okay, I believe I remember saying you like Matthew McConaughey films?"

He ran two of his fingers lightly across her forearm. She squirmed at the touch. "So beautiful," he said. "I see the goosebumps where I touch you. Skin. Such a fascinating organ—you know skin is an organ, right?"

She lay next to him, looking into his eyes without saying a word.

"Right?"

She nodded and smiled. "I do know that. And you have made mine quite excited."

He reached over and ran the back of his hand over her cheek. "Skin. It protects us. It transmits information about temperature, pressure, humidity. It releases moisture to cool us down."

He ran his finger down her neck and across her collarbone. She let out a small moan. It had been so long.

"Do you know what a fillet knife is?" He smiled. "My dad gave my mom's favorite one to me after she died. She used it for forty-three years. I was so moved, I cried." He pursed his lips. She reached up and cupped his face with a hand as he spoke. "The amount of flesh she has filleted with it."

He leaned down and kissed her. So soft. So warm. Her entire body responded—skin, heart, stomach, genitals. Her tongue found his. He shifted around and placed his forearm across her right wrist, holding it against the bed. She moaned again. He flipped one leg over both her thighs and pressed down.

This is really going to happen, she thought. It's only our second date, but this feels so right—

He reached back behind him and something scraped on the nightstand. "Here it is." He held up an old fillet knife. The wood handle was worn from decades of use. The blade shimmered, its sharp edge gleaming in the dim light.

She frowned.

"Skin," he said. "The largest organ of the body. Like the skin of a salmon, it can be removed and you can keep living." He raised his head a bit. "For a while."

He put his hand over her mouth as she struggled. Her muffled scream made him laugh as he lay the knife on her upper arm.

So Long

Lino looked down the old road toward Padova. The Italian countryside stretched out on all sides, a pale green plain dotted with patches of yellow. Silent. Still. Cold. Clear. A usual winter day in northern Italia.

His worn shoes made a grinding sound in the gravel as he turned in the opposite direction loud in the stillness. Ahead lay the town of Vicenza—a town he had never visited, despite its proximity. The road was almost a mirror of the view behind: a shabby pavement, stretching into the distance, the same pale winter farmlands spread out on either side. An occasional clump of trees and sections of old stone walls.

To the right, far off at the top of a slight rise was a stone farmhouse and a barn. It might be abandoned. Ruins. Or it perhaps it was full of life in the cold, clear afternoon. From this distance, Lino could not know. Death and life looked the same.

He turned to his left, breaking the silence with his shoes again. Train tracks, stretching away straight and true. Telephone poles stood next to the trees, closer to the tracks, spaced at even intervals. Each subsequent totem seemed smaller than the previous until they disappeared in miniature. A straight line of planted trees was a windshield between each set of poles. A neat, ordered geometry. Two straight iron rails receding until they touched. Wooden crossties at precise intervals. The spaced telephone poles and trees. Lino counted how many trees had been planted between the two poles closest to him. Thirteen. He counted the next set, and the next: as many as he could until the distance made it impossible to see. Each numbered thirteen. Order—and superstition be damned.

Lino turned a fourth time, one hundred and eighty degrees. Crunch. Once again, a mirror of the opposite direction, except, in the distance, the tracks curved around rising hills, the line of trees hiding the poles after the curve. He could only count three poles (thirty-nine trees).

Standing in the middle of the street and the middle of the tracks where the two crossed, Lino imagined what he looked like from far above. A small, insignificant dot, standing at the center of a cross made of wood, iron, and dirt. He raised his arms up from his sides. He knew that one of his arms was longer than the other, one was stronger than the other. His hair was combed to the side. The left pocket of his coat had some bread and cheese in it. An uneven geometric figure in the midst of a straight, ordered geometry. An unplanned flaw in the midst of the planned crossing. "A strange disfigurement standing at the cross," he said aloud. His voice startled him. It was loud and rough, as if it did not belong. Unfitting.

Why *do* people think everything must be nice and neat and structured? Why not unordered? Why can't disorder have meaning? Why can't the nasty and the disheveled and the dirty and the chaotic have a function? He knew the answer: order was important because it offered a sense of security. Clear boundaries. *This* is where one thing ends and another begins. Beginnings. Endings. Crucial to the human mind.

He turned and walked to the edge of the road where the tracks left the asphalt and continued on their long straight path. He examined the iron of the left-hand rail. It was quite worn. Where one section of rail fitted to another, it was slightly uneven. The rivets were leaning outward and looked a bit loose. If someone failed to check this and repair it, there would be a derailment. How long? How long before it caused a disaster? How many trains must fly by, loosening the rivets a tiny bit each time until it crossed the line to disaster? He imagined a train, speeding along at 187 kilometers per hour. All the passengers (the lucky ones in Prima classe) on just another run, just another trip, just another day. Suddenly, a bang! and a lurch! and rending and crashing and screeching. Who would survive? Who would be killed? How many merely maimed?

A sudden rustling sound. An animal in the brush. A bird. Or a rat. Lino stepped out onto the wooden cross-tie of the track. It was firm beneath his feet. He walked forward between the rails and stood on the next cross-tie. Then the third. And the fourth. On the seventh, he stopped and bent down to examine the gravel piled between the cross-ties. Each rock roughly the size of a large walnut. All the same grayish color.

He picked up a handful and felt the coldness. Squeezing his palm, the edges of the stones dug into his hands and fingers. He turned his hand upside down and released his grip, allowing gravity to create a lithic drizzle.

Where did these rocks come from? Is there a factory that turns them out by the tons, made for this function? Created for one purpose. Maybe someone checks them for quality. Another has them loaded into large containers and ships them off. Others place them between the ties. Not too many, not too few. Everything according to a plan, to the rules of train track construction. All worked out ahead of time. So nice and neat.

Lino looked to the side and saw one of the stones to the side of the rails, lying in the dirt at the bottom of the brief incline below the track mound. A rebellious rogue stone! Or perhaps a misfit! He stepped across the iron rail, down the little incline, and stood on the dirt punctuated with a few brown weeds and bits of green poking up here and there.

He stopped before the lone rock. How did it get here? Did an animal pick it up and drop it? Maybe, when they were laying the gravel, it had slipped off the pile and rolled here. Or perhaps a worker tossed it for fun. Or it had some defect that only a well-trained track-laying expert would know.

Now, it was just a plain rock.

Lino wondered what difference it made that it was here and not there. It no longer performed its function. It was just a rock. Not even a real rock. A manufactured rock, a pseudo-rock. It didn't belong here with genuine rocks and pebbles.

He raised his eyes once more and looked down the track. About fifteen or twenty meters ahead, on the left, was a low concrete wall. He had not noticed it before. How did it fit into the order universe of the locomotive industry? He walked to it, curious. He wondered why he was curious. What difference did it make?

He observed that the wall, about ten meters long, had been built because a small stream ran under the tracks through a corrugated culvert. The wall held back the piles of dirt and gravel which made up the bed for the tracks. How nice and neat. Just a long, large pipe, buried under the rails, with a wall to keep the bank steady. When the rains come, when the snows melted, the drainage could flow as if tracks had never bisected the land. The trains would speed across the plain and the passengers need never know of the stream.

He looked at his watch. He took a deep breath. It was warmer now, but it still had that cool crisp characteristic that hurt his lungs. He turned his head and listened. So silent. But not for long. The stillness would soon be broken by a deep and steady whooshing and a clacking of metal on metal that would build in volume. The EC 86 EuroCity. He had ridden that same train many times. No smoking was allowed—there was not a smoking car like on most trains. Some passengers would complain about that, but Italians were getting more used to it. There was a *Bordrestaurant* where one could buy pricey snacks, drinks, beer, and wine. The train made many stops between the old, rustic, stone Venezia Santa Lucia train station on the Grand Canal and the modern, clean, metal-edged München station—its terminal destination.

He stepped up onto the top of the wall with some effort—it was over a meter high, and Lino was tired and hungry. He almost lost his balance, but caught himself by waving his arms. Balanced, he turned and looked across the tracks. This point of view offered no new perspective, though he could now see where the culvert exited, about ten meters past the far side of the tracks.

He still had the rock in his hand. The poor, misfit rock. He looked at the tracks below. If he tossed it down, right there, it could land right between the ties. If he then looked away and back, he probably wouldn't be able to find it. Returned to its world, it would live among its brothers and sisters, one among many, performing its duty without drawing any attention. A nice, neat, ordered existence. Just what is expected of rail line gravel.

Of course, his aim might be off. Maybe a funny bounce would cause it to career off the tracks again. Ha! thought Lino, what an irony.

Or maybe it would bounce onto a cross-tie. Sitting on the wood. So improper. Naked to the world. Maybe the train would come and the incredible speed would expel the rock.

Maybe this time it would break up into unrecognizable pieces, scattered about. Having begun with purpose in some factory, ended as small pebbles strewn about with no purpose. Beginnings and endings. Vital.

He balanced the stone. What would happen? Once again, his curiosity surprised him. Why did he care? It was a rock, one among thousands—millions!

A sound caught his attention. The train was approaching. He could already see the top of the engine. It was a long way off, but he knew how fast it was moving. The sound grew loud, a terrible dragon, destroying everything in its path.

He threw the rock as hard as he could over the tracks. He felt the concrete tremble beneath his feet, and he lost sight of the rock. It must have traveled quite a distance. It was unlikely that any human would ever see it again. He would be the last to give it a thought.

The change in the roaring of the train indicated that it was nearing the road he had crossed. He imagined he could feel the heat and wind as it approached. A beast of enormous power bearing down. It would arrive within seconds.

He closed his eyes. Beginnings and endings. So important.

The *controllore* inserted his key into the lock of the communications panel, smooth and swift. He opened the thin metal door and swung it open. He lifted the phone off the hook, and, with a well-practiced gesture, used the top of the receiver to flip the switch labeled "all cars." He pulled a notebook out from under his arm with his left hand and glanced at the page. Pressing the button on the phone, he knew that, at that moment, all the passengers on every car would stop whatever they were doing and listen.

"*Buon giorno*, may I have your attention? We stopped because the train has struck an object. There is no damage to the train, but we must wait the arrival Polizei. Once they have made their report, in about an hour, we will be on our way to Vicenza. The Bordrestaurant is open for your enjoyment. We are sorry for this interruption in your travels. *Grazie*."

So Rude[1]

The alarm sounded at 6:17. Hoffman rolled over, grabbed the device, and yanked it hard enough to pull the electric cord from the wall socket. The sound stopped, and he tossed it on the floor.

He swung his legs over to sit on the edge of the bed, stretching his arms out. He smiled. "Gonna be a *good* day," he said out loud. "Shower first." He took a quick one.

Gazing into the mirror after, he felt fresh and clean. His skin burned from the steel wool he uses as a loofah; his hair was smooth and soft from a mask he had put on and left for 10 minutes.

Maybe I should shave my head, he thought. Sure, he possessed a fine, thick, full head of hair. Shaving it would make people wonder. He cocked his head and tried to imagine how he would look. *Might be interesting.*

In any case, he needed to shave his face. He opened a canister of shaving cream and placed a dollop in the porcelain cup that he kept beside the sink. Adding a little hot water, he stirred it with the horsehair brush he had bought in Paris. Turning the water to the hottest setting, he soaked a hand

[1]This story was selected as one of the winners in the 2022 Riversong Short Story Contest, and is included in the volume *2022 Best Short Stories: Riversong Contest*, edited by Neela Tudurí-Kłepfisch and published by Riversong Books in August, 2022.

towel and held it over his face for two minutes. It burned like hell, but he held steady, his grunts of pain muffled by the towel.

After carefully shaving his face, peering into the mirror periodically to make sure he hadn't missed a single hair, he gazed again at himself. "No good!" He yelled at the visage before him. "Boring!"

He opened the cabinet door and pulled out small containers and tubes. Five minutes later, he had applied a bit of foundation, blush strategically placed on his high cheeks, and just a touch of lipstick to brighten up his pale lips a bit.

Too obvious?

"It's not worthwhile if people don't notice, idiot!" He yelled at himself. "You need some eyelash and eyebrow work!"

He kept staring for a few minutes, then abruptly turned the water back on and washed all the makeup off. After applying a skin serum, beard balm, and a 50 SPF lotion, he went to the walk-in closet. Scanning the racks, he smiled at the carefully arranged clothing by season, purpose, and color. Such order made him happy. Looking through the spring section for, work, black, he pulled out a suit. He hadn't worn it in a while—he only purchased it last year. After perusing the winter, work, blue section, he pulled a linen shirt from the rack and dressed. Glancing at himself in the mirror, he thought he looked nice…but not quite right. He took them off and put them in the dry-cleaning bin. Something caught his eye on a lower shelf. Reaching down, he extracted a maroon polo shirt and a pair of khaki pants. They were wrinkled pretty badly, and there was a light stain on the left-hand side of the shirt about halfway down. He nodded to himself with satisfaction.

In the kitchen, he stood before the sink, eating a granola bar and drinking a protein smoothie. The smoothie addressed his bodily needs, and he gulped it down. The granola bar tasted like wood chips with some sugar. He made a face with each bite, but finished it anyway.

As he tossed the wrapper in the trash, his eye caught a bottle of garlic-infused olive oil sitting out on the counter. He must have left it there last night when he made dinner. He picked it up, took off the lid, and took a sniff. Nice. The fresh, buttery scent of olive oil with a hint of spicy garlic. His brow furrowed, and he upended the bottle to place a few drops on his open palm. He rubbed his hands together and wiped his neck, inside his elbows, and wrists. He smiled and took a deep breath.

"Perfect."

He spotted his coworkers as soon as he entered the café. Sliding into the booth next to Carmen, he greeted them both.

"Sorry I'm late. Traffic."

"No problem, we haven't ordered yet."

A waiter appeared, and Hoffman nodded for Carmen and Paul to go first as he looked over the menu. When it came to his turn, he ordered black coffee, eggs over easy, and wheat bread with jam.

"Looking pretty casual today, Hoffman," Paul said. "Casual Friday?" He laughed.

Hoffman briefly considered his response. Paul was always making irritating comments on his manner of dress. He was either too dressy or not dressy enough. Or he would make fun of the color or the cut or the style.

He decided to play along.

"Is it Friday?" He laughed. "Been working so hard on this Powercraft project, I have no idea what day it is."

Carmen nodded along with the other two. "Yes, we've all been burning the midnight oil over that one. Be glad when it's done. Did your team finish with the write-up?"

They continue talking about the project until the waiter returned with their food. Hoffman cut a piece of egg with his fork and lifted it to his nose, taking a long sniff. He nodded in satisfaction and chewed slowly. Placing the fork carefully on the edge of the plate, he raised the coffee cup and took a sip.

He spit it back out into the cup and looked around the diner, spotting the waiter two tables over. "Hey! Waiter! This coffee is ice-cold! Get it out of here and bring me a hot one!"

Both Carmen and Paul jerked in their seats, looking embarrassed. The waiter raised a single finger, indicating he'd be right over. He finished up and approached. "Yes, sir?"

"This coffee is ice-cold. Do your job!" he yelled.

The waiter, looking both annoyed and worried, said, "Sorry, I'll take care of it." He picked up the cup and walked back into the kitchen.

"You better." Hoffman shook his head, looking at his coworkers. "Simplest job in the world. Cup of hot coffee. Can't even do it. Why would you two suggest this place?"

Carmen opened her mouth to respond, but nothing came out.

Paul looked at her and then Hoffman. "Shit, Hoffman, it's just coffee."

Hoffman looked steadily at him. "Is that the kind of thinking that got you that promotion last month? 'Don't worry about it, we can fix it?' I never thought you deserved that promotion anyway."

Paul was speechless. He looked at Carmen, who just grimaced. The waiter arrived with a steaming cup of coffee and placed it beside Hoffman.

Hoffman smiled, with a shy look on his face. "Thank you, sir. I apologize for my outburst, that was uncalled for. Sometimes I get cranky when I haven't had my coffee. Not your fault. Shake?" He held his hand.

"Oh…uh sure…" He held out his hand, and the two men shook. "Thank you."

"No problem, you didn't deserve that." Hoffman looked down at their hands and let go. "You have a strong, firm handshake. Well-manicured hands. That tells me you're a good man with refined tastes. Please accept my apology once more."

The waiter offered a confused smile. "Well, thank you, sir. Happy to serve. Let me know if you need anything else."

"Perfect, thank you. Now go take care of those people at that table, and offer them my apologies as well for interrupting their order." He turned back to the other two. Carmen's brow was furrowed. Paul was just staring at him. *Perfect.* Hoffman took a bite of toast.

"What the hell, Hoffman?" Paul said.

"You know," Hoffman replied, chewing thoughtfully. "This blueberry jam may be the best I have ever had." He swallowed and took a sip of the coffee. "Ah. Perfection."

He placed the coffee cup down, folded his hands in front of him, and looked at each of the other two. "I was wrong. This was an excellent choice for breakfast. And now that I think of it," he fixed Paul with a sympathetic expression, "you actually did deserve that promotion. Your work on the Kinderhaus account was exceptional." He cut a bit of egg and held it before his mouth. "I was just yanking your chain."

Paul looked at Carmen and shook his head. Carmen shrugged.

❖

He sauntered into his office and sat down at the large, polished wood desk and sighed. The surface was a study in contrasts. Some of it was neat. Papers stacked cleanly. A pen sitting on top of the stack at a perfect 45-degree angle. Three Post-it notes were arranged, one below the other to the left. The computer screen, keyboard, and touch device sat at exact parallel angles. Yet, there was a stack of miscellaneous sized papers, each having appeared to have been thrown down in the general direction of the others. A small pool of liquid on the desk—probably coffee—floated precariously close to the stack. Three or four granola bar wrappers scattered about. The phone was sitting cockeyed on a book like it had a flat tire.

He smiled. He took a deep breath and look around the room. Framed items—diplomas, awards, photos of a sailing trip he took in the Bahamas three years ago, and a variety of paintings. Some had been hung carefully, square with the room and aligned with others for maximum aesthetics. Others were cockeyed and hung either too low or too high. Two chairs in from of the desk were set facing directly at the desk, both aligned with the other. The couch against the far wall had worn leather sections, stains, and was piled with papers, books, and garbage.

He reached out to the keyboard and tapped a key, causing the computer monitor to come to life. After a while of reading and answering emails, he frowned. He picked up the keyboard and turned it over in his hands, shaking his head. Dropping it on the desk, he reached for the phone.

"IT. Matt speaking."

"Matt, this is Hoffman. I don't like the way this keyboard feels."

"Again? We've changed your keyboard three times this year. What's the problem?"

"I just don't like it. Affects my productivity."

He heard a sigh on the other end of the phone. "Well, we can keep trying different keyboards, but it would be helpful if you could tell me what it is you don't like, or what you do like. Is it the action? The size of the keys?"

"Don't know, as I said. I'm not a computer expert."

"So we just keep trying different ones until you find one you like?"

"Yes, you damn moron. Do your job!"

"Mr. Hoffman, you don't have to be so rude!"

"No problem, Matt. I am a patient man. Let's try a new one, and we'll see how it goes."

"Uh…okay…okay…I'll see what I have or order another, different—"

"Excellent! You're the best, Matt. Have a great day."

He hung up the phone and placed it back on the book, balanced, with one corner off, as before. A coffee cup caught his eye, behind the phone. He picked it up and looked inside. Brownish liquid. Probably left from Friday. He raised it to his lips and took a sip. Not bad. The cream had curdled, but it added an interesting twist. He downed the rest of it.

There was a knock at his door. "Come in," he said, as he set the empty cup down on its side.

Kate peeked her head in. "Here's your mail. Also, James wants to know if you're up for a meeting in thirty minutes.

Just him and you. He's on his way to the office." She walked across the room and set a pile of mail on the desk, bundled together with a rubber band.

"Sure, no problem. His office?"

" He didn't say. I'll find out and buzz you."

"Thanks."

As she turned to leave, Hoffman said, "What's that odor? Perfume?"

She dimpled. He knew she loved positive comments. "Yes, a new one."

"I like it. It suits you."

"Thank you! Have a good morning, I'll buzz you in a minute. Door open or closed?"

"Leave it open."

He turned back to his computer, looking at his schedule for the rest of the week. He needed to finish a presentation before Wednesday, for the meeting about the Palmerson project. Probably should work on that today after the meeting with—the phone buzzed and he jumped. He hated the sound of these phones. He had repeatedly asked IT to set up a different, less abrasive sound for the phones. They treated his request like a minor inconvenience.

He reached over and picked up the phone with both hands. Raising it over his head, he flung it with great force at the open door. As it flew, the momentum ripped the cable out of the socket on the floor. He watched with pleasure as it smashed into the wall on the other side of the hall. A satisfying dent in the sheet rock made him smile.

Carl, who worked in the office next to his, stuck his head in tentatively. "Everything okay?"

"Always. I just don't like the ringtone. How is your day going? How was your weekend?"

"Um…" He stepped through the doorway. "Good. Good. Janet and I finally took the kids on that camping trip."

"That sounds great. I have a few moments, if you do, I'd love to hear about it."

Carl frowned, and took two slow steps into the office, one slow step at a time. "Okay, yes…sure…"

Hoffman jumped up. "Let me clear a space on the couch, and you can tell me all about it!"

About mid-morning, he felt pangs of hunger. He headed downstairs to the little café in the office industrial building, ordering his usual: a bagel with cream cheese. As he re-entered the elevator, he saw there was a woman inside. Hoffman didn't know her, so he nodded, still chewing on his bagel, and punched the button for his floor. It didn't light up. He pushed again. Still nothing.

"Dammit! What's wrong with the maintenance in this place! What a fucking tragedy!"

The woman standing beside him gasped, and then recovered and said: "We're moving, the button works, just the light is out, I guess."

He noticed that the elevator was going up. "Well, you're right. It just goes to show you we shouldn't jump to conclusions!" He gave her a smile. "Are you having a nice day so far?"

"Uh, yes. Going fine."

He enjoyed elevator rides. Such a strange occasion. Until the elevator was invented, no such social interaction existed where several strangers packed together in a little metal box, riding up and down in total silence.

The elevator stopped at floor three and two other people got on, talking, but once the doors closed they stopped and stared straight ahead. At floor four, three people got on, and took up the requisite stance.

"Wow, someone in here stinks!" Hoffman felt satisfaction as every person jumped. He turned to look at each person, then focused on a smallish man with spectacles and an ill-fitting and disheveled suit. "Is it you? You seem as if you're not good at hygiene. Phew!" He made a face.

The man opened his mouth and then closed it, his face turning red. The woman who had entered with the man spoke up. "That's not very nice!"

"You think not?" Hoffman turned his attention to her. "You're standing beside him; surely you smell it?"

"I don't smell anything, in fact, I think he smells very nice, and I think you are so rude."

Hoffman turned the corners of his mouth down. "Do you?" He pursed his lips, thinking. "Yes, I think you are probably right." He turned back to the small man. "My apologies, sir, what I'm smelling is not you. Perhaps it is my upper lip!" He laughed, and some of the others laughed also, albeit with some awkwardness.

He turned back to the woman. "Let's change the subject." He could almost feel the tension as they waited to hear what he would say next. "You would certainly agree with me that the lighting is not good in here, correct? Whoever invented fluorescent lighting should be shot. Although, now that I think of it, the inventor is probably dead by now."

The woman glanced at him and around at the others, as if she was unsure what to say. One of the other men on the other side of the elevator spoke. "Yes, I've always hated fluorescent lighting. Makes you look sickly."

"It makes me look sickly?" Hoffman said to him, with a frown. "I *have* been feeling under the weather lately. Perhaps I should go to the doctor. What do you think?" he said to the woman he had been talking to.

At the same time, the elevator arrived at his floor. "Ah, this is me." He stepped off and turned back as the doors closed. "Thank you for an enjoyable ride, everyone, I've learned something, and I hope you all have a fantastic day."

He stepped into the pub and scanned the room for Rodrigue. Spotting him at a bar table in the corner, he made his way over.

"Hey, Rodrigue, how are you doing today?"

Rodrigue looked up, sliding his fingers through his long bangs, to push them away, as he often did. "Pretty well. You?"

"Ah, just a day. Nothing good, nothing bad." He took the other seat. "Nice jacket! Is it new?"

"It is. I just got it at Nordstrom's. Needed to get a new one for the conference in Philadelphia next month."

"Very classy, it suits you well. Pun intended."

A waiter came over and asked if he could take their order. Rodrigue ordered a pub burger and a red ale.

"Here's what I would like," Hoffman said. "I want your spicy chili shrimp, but I want it extra spicy. And I mean slap-your-mother spicy. And bring me to Newcastle Ale, and a bottle of Tabasco and Sriracha if you have it."

The waiter nodded and left. Music began playing somewhere, a piano. Hoffman looked about with surprise, spotting a piano and the player. "God, I hate piano music," he said, speaking entirely too loud. "I don't know why anyone would want to play the piano. Shit for brains, I guess, and garbage for talent."

Rodrigue leaned forward. "Keep your voice down a bit, huh?"

"Just wanted to make sure you hear me over that racket. And I don't care if the piano player hears me, he's got to be an utter moron."

Rodrigue furrowed his brow, searching Hoffman's face. The waitress delivered their beers, and both sipped from the pint glasses.

"Ah…" Hoffman breathed. "So good."

Rodrigue set his glass down. "How was your day? Anything new going on?"

Hoffman took another deep gulp before answering. "It was fine. The usual. Mostly, I love my job. The people are great. In all departments! That's gotta be unusual, yes?"

His friend nodded. "Yes, I don't suppose—"

"Oh yeah," Hoffman nodded enthusiastically. "Even today—had to call IT for a new keyboard. Those guys are *so* helpful. Always." His eyes went distant for a brief moment. "I'm probably a pain in their ass, but still, always nice, always helpful. Good stuff."

The waiter arrived and placed the plates before each of them. He pulled a bottle of Sriracha and Tabasco out of his apron pockets and set them beside Hoffman's plate. "Is there anything else I can get you gentlemen?"

Rodrigue shook his head, but Hoffman spoke. "Yes, I wonder…could your chef chop up a bunch of jalapeño peppers for me?"

"On the side?"

"Of course." The waiter nodded and left. Hoffman looked at Rodrigue's plate. "That's the pub burger and fries?"

"Yes. One of my favorite dishes there. I order it every time."

"Hm. Hadn't noticed." Hoffman reached across the table and took a French fry. Rodrique sat up straight with a questioning look. "Not bad, not bad. Appears to be house made—see the way the fries are all cut differently?"

"Yes, of course, but you should ask before—"

Hoffman reached across and picked up the untouched burger with one hand. He held it before him and examined the side. He took the top bun off and looked at it, nodding approvingly. "Might have to try this sometime." He took a bite. Rodrigue opened his mouth, then closed it as Hoffman replaced the burger on his plate.

"Mmmm. Cooked to perfection. Not many places can do that. Might have to try this sometime." He picked up the bottle of Sriracha, unscrewed the lid, and shook it upside down all over the spicy shrimp plate. He did the same with the bottle of Tabasco. When the waiter returned with a small bowl of jalapeños, he dumped them all over the dish. He looked up a Rodrigue. "You going to eat?"

Rodrigue smiled slightly. "In a moment."

Hoffman took his plate with both hands and lifted it to his face, taking a deep, long sniff. "Ah…smells like disaster. Let's do this." He put it down and began stuffing shrimp after shrimp in his mouth, hardly finishing chewing one before beginning on another. After a moment he stopped, blowing air repeatedly like he was in labor. "Wow, that is something else. Probably make me sick for days!" He laughed, and Rodrigue noticed that beads of sweat had appeared on his brow and above his upper lip.

"Hoffman, may I ask you a question? It's personal, so you don't have to answer."

"Beer doesn't really help with this kind of heat, you know? Sure, ask away. We've been friends for over a year now, I think. Personal is okay."

"Do you have some form of Turret's?"

Hoffman laughed. "No. Not at all. Why?"

"I don't know—just seems like you often engage in behavior that is unusual, perhaps extreme, and some people might say rude. Yet, you are one of the kindest people I know. I can't figure it out."

His friend wiped his mouth with a napkin, leaving a blood-colored stain behind. He made three more blowing noises, then picked the napkin back up and blew his nose into it.

"Wow. This may be the hottest dish I've ever had. Compliments to the chef." He chuckled. "Thanks for the compliment. No Turrets Syndrome for me. Just living and enjoying life, my friend. Just enjoying life."

Rodrique finally picked up his burger, turning it away from the bite already taken.

Hoffman tossed his keys in the bowl beside the door and took off his shoes where he stood. He went to the kitchen and poured himself a bourbon, neat.

Leaning back on the couch, he let a heavy sigh escape his lips. He held up the glass, tilting it one way and another, staring at the dark amber liquid. Bringing it to his lips, he took two generous sips.

"Oh, yes," he whispered to himself. He took another sip, then leaned forward, elbows on hands, both hands holding the glass in front of him.

"Oh God, help me feel something. *Something*!"

He drained the rest of his drink, setting it down a bit too forcefully on the coffee table. He dropped to the floor on his hands and knees, sobbing.

He went into the bathroom and splashed water on his face from the sink faucet. He took the soap and washed his face, splashed some more, then dried it with a hand towel.

Back in the kitchen, he poured another dram of bourbon. He sat down at the little desk at the other end of the kitchen and pulled out a piece of paper and begin writing.

1. Ask Marty how his meeting went

2. Get some flowers on the way to work for Kate, whose mother passed away last weekend.

3. Find a homeless person and take them to lunch.

4. Starbucks gift cards for Matt in IT, Carmen, Paul, and Rodrigue.

He sat back at the couch, and switched on the television with the remote. A correspondent was reporting from the war. A bomb had hit a hospital. The physical and economic toll of the war on the civilians was devastating. The correspondent turned to an interviewee, a military medic. The man's uniform was disheveled, and he had a smudge of something on his cheek, up near his eye. Hoffman spotted blood on his sleeve as he gestured, talking about the dreadful conditions. He squinted at the screen, trying to read the platoon patch on the medic's shoulder.

For a brief moment, his eyes lost focus, and he stared off into space. Abruptly, he turned off the television, and stood, eyes welling with tears. Wiping them away, he arose and poured a third glass of bourbon. He held the bottle up. It was almost empty. He poured the rest into the glass, nearly to the brim, and tossed the bottle into the garbage. Sipping as he went, he moved to stand before a small display table in the living room. Pictures and knickknacks were situated carefully on the surface. He gazed at the pictures. One of his dad, two of his mom, one of his sister and his brother.

The tears began to flow again. He looked up at the framed letters on the wall. Four of them. All the beginning with the words, "Posthumous commendations have been awarded to…"

He drained the last of his drink and placed it in the kitchen sink. In the bedroom, he picked up the alarm clock from the floor and set it back on the bedside table. The electric plug tines were bent, so he forced the bent plug tines back into shape and plugged it in. He checked his watch and then set the time.

He set the alarm for 6:17 and crawled into bed, pulling the sheet over his head.

So Snowy

She had walked past him three times already. He did not notice her, though she had walked in front of the bench where he sat.

Her mother called out. "Mandy! Quit running off!" She took her hand. "What are you doing?"

"Mom," she hissed. "I think that's Santa."

"Santa is on the lower level, honey. Do you want to see him? You said you were too old."

"Not the *pretend* Santa." She pulled her mother's arm. "_Him_." She pointed back at the man.

Her mom turned to gaze at the old man on the bench. She smiled. "Oh, his beard *is* so snowy. But no red suit." She frowned. "And he doesn't seem too jolly."

Mandy pulled away. "Maybe he's sad Christmas is over and nobody will think of him 'til next year."

"Well, I don't think anybody forgets Santa. Besides, Santa spends all year with his elves and Mrs. Santa making the toys for the next year." Her phone rang, and as she raised it to her ear, Mandy took the opportunity to slip away again.

She positioned herself right in front of the man, at a cautious five-foot distance. His eyes, a deep blue, lost their unfocused stare and peered at the little girl.

"Are you Santa Claus?" she asked.

The question seemed to confuse him at first. Then he raised one corner of his mouth. "No." He shook his head. "I'm not Santa Claus."

"Then why is your beard so long and so snowy?"

"Lots of people have white beards."

"Are you married?"

His eyes lost focus. "Not any more."

She considered the answer for a moment. "Do you have helpers?"

"Not anyone who works for me, if that's what you mean."

"What do you do? Where do you live?"

He chuckled. "You're full of questions, aren't you?"

She nodded. "Daddy says that asking questions is how we learn and get smart."

"A wise man. Is your dad here?"

"No, he lives in Oklahoma. I was supposed to go see him over Christmas vacation, but my brother got sick and Mom had to pay like *five hundred dollars* to get him well."

"I'm sorry. Is your brother okay?"

"He's okay. I thought he was faking it to get out of school, but he was in the hospital for three days. I think Mom was scared, except she told me everything would be fine."

"Where is your mom?" He looked up. "Ah, I suspect this is her coming along now."

"I'm so sorry she's disturbing you, sir. Mandy, don't bother people when they're sitting quietly. Come along."

"She's not bothering me."

Mandy's mom smiled. "I'm sure she's pestering you with questions. Come along, Mandy." She took the little girl's hand. "Have a pleasant afternoon, sir. Happy New Year."

The man watched as the two walked away. Mandy kept looking back.

"Wait," he called out, "I'd like to give you something, Mandy." He glanced at her mom. "If that's okay with you."

Mandy looked up at her mother with puppy-dog eyes. Her mother nodded. "Go ahead."

Mandy came to stand in front of the old man. He looked at her for a moment, smiling.

"I'm not Santa. But I have been known to give presents." He reached into a pocket in his large jacket and pulled out a small, tattered box. "Here you go. Now run along with your mom."

Beaming, she took the box, and with a thank you, ran back to her mom. "See?! I *told* you he was Santa."

Her mother frowned. "Let me see."

Mandy handed her the box. Her mom stopped to open it, and gasped. "Oh, Mandy, I'm sorry, we can't accept this." She fanned through the bills. "This is five hundred dollars!"

She looked back, but the bench was empty.

So Sweet

"Ah, so sweet."

I frowned. "What, Grampa?"

"Croissants. Chocolate croissants." He grunted as he adjusted his café chair. "So tasty. I love a sweetmeat."

"Yes, they are. But you ordered the almond croissant, not the chocolate."

"Did I?" His brow furrowed.

"Would you like me to exchange it?"

He waved a thin hand. "No, no. Almond is tasty, too. A fine sweetmeat."

"Why are you calling them 'sweetmeats?'"

"Oh, I've always called them sweetmeats."

I'd never heard him call them that, although we come here and get croissant and coffee weekly. Besides, I thought sweetmeats were candies, not pastries. I pulled out my phone by reflex and spoke the command to search for it.

"Are you sure you don't want me to get you a chocolate croissant instead?"

"No, Laura, it's really fine." He looked around. "They sure are taking their sweet time with the coffee, though."

The irritation that had crept into his voice bothered me, but not as much as the name. "Grampa, I'm Dahlia. Laura is my sister."

He smiled. "Dahlia. Now there's a sweet girl. I wonder what she's doing these days."

We had this same conversation every time. When I corrected him, he said the same thing. Every. Single. Day.

I looked down at my phone.

Sweetmeat. (n). An item of confectionery or sweet food. Archaic.

Well, he got that right, at least. I smiled at the tag next to the definition. That described grampa, too. His cane, hat, shirt, manner of speaking—all archaic. Which was okay. Even adorable in an elderly person.

The barista called my name. "I'll get them, Grampa."

I went to the counter and picked up the two cups and went to take a sip of one. The girl stopped me.

"That one is for him." She nodded at my grampa.

I frowned. "Aren't they the same?"

She smiled. "His has something a little special—he's a VIP. Such a sweet man."

I returned her smile and took the cups. "Thank you." That was nice. Glad to see they think of him fondly.

I returned to the table and set his cup in front of him.

He took a sip, returned the cup to its saucer with both hands. "Dahlia? Isn't Laura going to meet us?"

"No, Grampa. She lives in Kentucky, remember?"

He frowned. "What? I…" His hand trembled as he looked off into the distance. His left eye was cloudier than usual. He grimaced.

I leaned forward to hold his hand. "What is it?"

He shook his head and focused back into the present. My heart slowed. "Nothing, dear. Just…I thought she told us she'd meet us here. Last night she said…" He shook his head again and fixed me with a sad smile. "I'm not remembering, am I?"

I squeezed his hand and smiled back. "No, but that's okay. We all do that sometimes."

Mom had told me not to pretend as if it was okay. It made it worse, she said. Acknowledge his memory problems, then help him know it's all right not to remember when you have a disease.

I couldn't do it.

He took another sip and sighed. "Ah, so sweet."

We came here to give Mom some time to herself or to run errands or whatever. I'd pick him up from the house, and we'd walk to this café. It seemed good for him.

And me.

We drank coffee and ate pastries, had the same conversations as if they were new. Then we'd walk to the park and sit for a while, watching children or dogs or birds. Back at the house, we'd watch a television show or read, and wait for Mom to come home.

"Grampa, I want to remind you. I won't be here next week, I'm going up to Roanoke." I knew he wouldn't remember, but it seemed important to keep having normal conversations. Maybe it was only important for me.

He looked up. "Oh? Roanoke? What for?" The same words as last time.

"I'm visiting an old friend. We try to get together once every few months."

"Ah. That's fine, just fine. Good to have friends." He looked off again with that vacant stare. I hated it.

"Yes," I said, with a little more animation. "I'm going to take the train."

He returned to me. "The train? Oh, I love the train." He took another sip. "You know, once, when I was about fifteen, a friend of mine and I decided to explore the train tracks outside our town. This was outside Fredericksburg…about the mid-1930s."

I did the math in my head. He was right.

"He and I—his name was Paul—started walking down the tracks. We got about a mile outside town where the tracks went across a train bridge. This was in the old days: a wooden bridge, no railing." He leaned back and cackled a bit. "Oh, we thought we were such adventurers. Walking across the ties, we could see down into the gorge below. Perhaps 75 feet!"

I'd never heard this story, and I was pretty sure it was not true. Maybe he'd read it somewhere, or saw it in a movie. That happened a lot with his memories.

"That seems dangerous."

He caught my eye. "Oh, yes. The unthinking ways of youth, yes? The myth of immortality!"

I was surprised at the change in his manner of his speech. More clarity. Longer sentences.

"To continue the story: we get about halfway across the bridge and we hear a train whistle behind us. Paul yelled, 'run!' We take off—across these open railroad ties, mind you —and I look back to see a train approaching the bridge. Oh, my heart was a-pounding!"

Now I was sure this wasn't true. But the way he was telling it captured me. "Grampa! Obviously, you made it, but it must have been scary!"

"Oh, yes. When we got home, mother forbid me to have anything to do with Paul for weeks after that!" He leaned forward. "The truth is, Dahlia, it was my idea. Oh, I felt so bad. But I couldn't bring myself to tell her." He took another sip and sighed. "Yes, we made it to the other side, almost diving off the tracks onto the bank. Perhaps my memory fails me, but the train flew by, sounding its whistle, seconds after we left the tracks."

I smiled. It was a good story, and it obviously gave him pleasure to tell it. Maybe that's all that mattered.

"Mr. Lewing?" A middle-aged man stood slightly behind and beside me.

My grandfather looked up. "Yes, I am he?" He looked a bit confused. I cringed inside. This happened sometimes—people from the neighborhood, or a store, or someone he'd known. He rarely remembered, even with prompting. Then I had to explain. As Grampa sat right there. So embarrassing.

"I thought so! I'm James. You were my teacher in high school!"

Grampa squinted his eyes. "James. James." He slapped the table. "James Portos! I remember—you had a lot of trouble as a freshman, but became an honor student by graduation."

"Thanks to you, sir! Your tutoring after school made the difference. How are you doing?"

"I am doing quite well." He looked at me. "This is my granddaughter, Dahlia. She works at the Government Center in HR. But more than that, she's a wonderful person."

James shook my hand. "Pleasure to meet you, Dahlia." He turned back. "I am sure she is wonderful if related to you." He nodded. "I won't disturb you further, I just wanted to say hello."

"I'm glad you did, James. Have a pleasant day, and maybe I'll see you again."

I was stunned. Sure, in his earlier stages of dementia, Grampa had moments of clarity and memory like that. But not in years.

"Grampa…you remembered him?"

He took the last sip of his coffee. "I didn't recognize his face—it's been a long time! But once he said his name, it all came back to me." He nodded to himself. "Sweet kid."

I nodded, not sure what to say.

"I'm not totally senile, you know, Dahlia." He cackled.

I laughed with him, but remembered the doctor's words to the contrary a few months ago.

"Hey, you two!" It was my mom.

"Mom? Why are you here? It's your day off."

She hugged her dad from the side. "I told you this morning. Your grandfather has a doctor's appointment at noon."

"You did? I don't remember that."

"I do," Grampa said, with a twinkle in his eye. "She told you right as we were leaving."

What was going on?

"Listen, Dad, we need to go. I'd like to stop by the dispensary first." She turned back to me. "Dahlia, would you mind getting me a coffee while I get him settled in the car?"

"Uh, sure mom, no problem…regular with sweet cream, right? Um…can I ask you something first?" I stood and nodded her away from the table. She frowned and followed me.

As we got out of earshot, she said, "Everything okay?"

"Oh, yes, yes, fine. Just that…well, Grampa told me a story I never heard. About him and a friend running across a train bridge to escape an oncoming train?"

She laughed. "Ah, yes, that was a family story from when he was a kid! He and his best friend, Paul. I remember my grandmother bringing that up whenever she wanted to poke at him."

"So it really happened?"

"As far as I as know. I mean, I heard it first from my mom and my grandmother—his mom—when I was a little girl. Why?"

I shook my head. "Just never heard it before."

"Ah, you thought it was one of his confused memories. I'm surprised you hadn't ever heard it before, at least when Grandma was alive."

I shrugged. "Maybe I forgot. I'll get your coffee."

She went to put Grampa in the car, and I ordered her coffee. When I took it to the parking lot, Grampa was in the passenger seat and mom was buckling his seatbelt. I handed the coffee to her and leaned down into the car as she went around to the driver's side.

"I enjoyed our time, Grampa. See you next week!"

He jumped and looked up in a bit of a panic.

"Oh, sorry, Grampa, I didn't mean to surprise you!"

He looked back forward, staring through the windshield. "It's okay, Laura. Are we going to have coffee today?"

I frowned. "Uh…we just finished. And I'm Dahlia." It came out starker than I intended.

A moment of confusion passed over his face. "Oh, yes, that's right." He looked sad. I put my hand on his shoulder.

"It's okay, Grampa. We all forget sometimes." My mom flashed me an expression of disapproval. "Love you." I kissed him on the cheek. "Bye, Mom. Let me know if you need anything."

"Bye, sweetheart."

As they drove off, I stood in the parking lot, lost in thought.

I returned to the coffee shop and approached the barista.

"How can I help you? A latte? One of our special iced coffees?" The girl said.

"No—I mean, I have a question. The other barista, the one who prepared our coffees earlier. Can I talk to her?"

"Who was it?"

"I didn't see her name, but she has short brown hair, a little shorter than you. Glasses, I think."

She frowned. "We don't have anyone here who looks like that."

"What? She waited on me. Gave us our drinks. Said she made my grandfather's coffee special for him. Are you sure?"

She laughed. "More than sure. We have a standing joke that all the baristas here are either blonde or ginger. Anything else?"

I shook my head and walked out. I wandered around the parking lot for ten minutes before I remember that we had walked here.

So Tired

The bed creaked. The frame was old—well over fifty years. The mattress, the box springs, and bedclothes were old too, though not as old as the bed. Well worn to the point of comfort, but not to the point of ruin. It was sturdy, but it showed its age in both style and the way it creaked when the owner stirred.

The occupant rolled over towards the nightstand. Creak. Not an alarming creak. A homey, comfortable creak. Like the floorboards of an old, warm house, full of memories from a good life.

The alarm sounded. A modern sound in contrast to the rustic creak. The man moaned. After a loud sigh, he heaved himself to a sitting position and reached over to silence the alarm. Three different parts of the bed creaked again, in unison, and the bed frame swayed a bit as he swung his legs to the side and stood. He took a deep breath, then turned back to gaze at the covers. *I need to make the bed. I don't think I have done it in a week.* He stood for a moment longer, gazing down with sleepy eyes. *I'll do it after a bite to eat.*

After breakfast, he took a shower in the adjoining bathroom. A square of autumn sunlight crept along the floor towards the bed. By the time he dried off, the light was halfway up the footboard. Had he noticed, the sunlight had worked for many years on the wood: uneven fading, varnish thin or gone, cracks and scrapes long dried out.

He strode into the room as he strapped on his watch, grimacing at the late hour. The cat wandered in from the hallway. *I need to feed you before I go! Late again.* He grabbed the wayward pillows and threw them at the headboard. *Damn, I don't have time for this. Tonight when I get home. I'll just make a chore of it and change the sheets. How long has it been? Maybe five or six days.* He rushed out of the room, oblivious to the meowing.

He shuffled through the door and switched on the lamp beside the bed. The room lit up. *Ugh. I was going to change the sheets tonight.* He paused. *Where is the other set? Did I wash them?* He tossed the plastic bag he was carrying onto the bed, spilling its contents onto the crumpled sheets: a bar of soap, a bottle of mouthwash, and a pack of razors. He left the room.

Two hours later he stumbled back into the room. He had gone down to discover the extra bedclothes clean but still in the dryer. He took them to the living room to disentangle them and turned on the TV. A basketball game caught his attention, he watched while drinking a half of a bottle of rum. Coming awake with a start, he saw the game was over, and the announcers were recapping. He stumbled to his room, fumbled with the covers, and was snoring in a matter of moments.

Around 1:00 a.m. he awoke, staggered to the bathroom, came back, switched off the lamp, and fell back into bed with a groan.

The alarm had been sounding for thirty minutes before he woke up. He groaned and rolled over. It took a few moments before he could focus well enough to read the clock. *Oh, shit!* He jumped up, got caught in the bedclothes, and went down in a heap on the floor.

His head ached, the inside of his mouth was a sticky mess, and his stomach was protesting. *I have to stop doing this every night.* He put in many hours at work, and he was superb at his job. No one would care if he didn't come in for this one day. But it was a source of pride: he was the best at what he did. Responsibility and doing one's best made for a valuable human being. He wasn't going to screw that up.

He extricated himself from the bedclothes and rose to his feet. Walking caused him to wince at the pain in his head. He stood under the hot water in the shower, almost passing out from the warmth and relation.

Back in the bedroom, he rummaged around in the bedclothes to find the bag of items he had brought home. Opening the sealed plastic around the bottle of mouthwash was a struggle. He took a swig. Some of it spilled on the mattress and the bedclothes, which were lying half on the floor.

"Argggh!!" He shook his head violently, then grimaced at the pain. He set the bottle down in the nightstand without the lid.

As he finished dressing, he realized how hot it was in the room. He went to the French-style window and flung it open. Cool air wafted in. A crisp autumn morning. He took a deep breath. Much better. *I have to check the air conditioner this evening.* He leaned out the window and reached out to touch some of the leaves of the large tree outside the window. Fresh. Alive. Nice.

The house stood silent and empty for many hours. The sun set. It had been a cool, clear day, but the weather began to turn as the afternoon waned. The temperature dropped. The autumn wind began to blow, swirling around the house and gusting through the open window in the bedroom every few moments. His cat was curled up on the bed because the back door had never been opened. Darkness descended within moments as the storm clouds grew thick.

A few autumn leaves, casting about in the wind, fluttered into the room and alighted on the bed and floor. Startled, the cat leaped from the bed and sped from the room. It began to rain. Had anyone been there to listen, they would have heard the pitter-patter on the sidewalk and roof. Soon, it became a downpour.

The room was clothed in the late afternoon light coming in through the window. Stomping feet announced someone coming up the stairs. The lights came on, and a figure walked to the bed and sat down on the edge with a loud thump. A deep breath, and then a long sigh. *I am so tired. And I don't feel too well.* He turned his head to view himself in the mirror which hung over the dresser. Pale. Filthy. He took off his cap, stained with dirt and sweat. His shirt was dark under the armpits from the strenuous work in the garden. He looked down at his jeans. From mid-calf down was a dark color—water had wicked up the legs from the wet yard. The bottom of each leg was crusted in mud so thick he could not even see the hems. His boots were also caked with mud. Some of the bedclothes had fallen onto the floor, and one boot was resting on it. He lifted his foot. *Ugh. I really have to wash these sheets now.*

A wave of nausea hit him. He ran into the bathroom, leaving boot-shaped mud prints. A few moments later he shuffled out, wiping his mouth. He groaned. *Maybe some soup. Or crackers.* He lurched out the door.

He returned with a box of crackers and a can of soda and eased himself onto the bed, swinging his feet up and bracing his back against the headboard. The wood protested.

Boots. He set the crackers and the soda aside, and, with some effort, leaned forward, one foot towards his chest, pulling off one and then the other boot, tossing them to the floor. Slumping back—*creak*—he popped open the can and drank. After a few sips, he opened the box of crackers and ate a few. Dry. His mouth felt even more sickly. He tossed the box aside and drank the rest of the soda in a series of gulps. Better. The carbonation felt good.

So tired. So hot. He scrunched down to lay flat and balanced the can beside him. It fell over. A last bit of liquid seeped out onto the bedclothes. He was already breathing slow and methodically.

Monday morning arrived with an overcast sky, making it darker than usual at the time. The alarm began beeping. The figure on the bed rolled over and shut it off, lying still for a moment. *Better. My fever has stayed down since last night. Maybe I am over this.*

After a few moments, he rose to a sitting position and disentangled himself from the bedclothes. Creak. Swinging his legs over the side, he sat on the edge of the mattress. Creak. He took a slow, deep breath. *A whole Sunday in bed. More than twenty-four hours.* He remembered the fever, the sweating, throwing the bedclothes off, then shivering and pulling them back. *Have I eaten anything since Saturday night?* He didn't remember even getting up except to go to the bathroom. *Oh, yes, I went down and made some tea early Sunday morning. And fed the cat.* A dim dream.

He leaned over and set the alarm to the last possible moment he could get up and still arrive at work on time if he skipped breakfast. He lay back and was asleep almost instantly.

The alarm sounded, and he and was standing before he realized it. A few moments passed before he got his bearings. It came back to him: fever, sickness, lying in bed all night Saturday and all day Sunday. He felt much better now, though weak. He peered at the clock. There was time. He scuffled to the bathroom.

The room was dark. He stepped in and switched on the lamp beside the bed. He stopped.

Oh, my God.

The bedclothes looked like Gordian himself had come and tied them. Half off the bed, they were stained and dirty. *How long has it been since I changed them?*

A movement under the sheet caused him to jump before he realized it was the cat.

"What are you doing there?! Did I not put you out?" The creature, at the sound of his voice, wriggled out from her hiding place and stalked towards him. He shooed her away, and then spotted a wet spot on the bed where she had relieved herself. He pulled the covers and sheet the rest of the way off. An empty can clattered to the floor. Leaves drifted lazily up and then down. The fitted sheet was just as dirty and pulled loose on one corner. Crumbs of food and dirt completed the disaster. The cover sheet itself looked like it had been exposed to the elements for months.

He gave a deep sigh. Reaching down, he pulled the edge of the fitted sheet from the mattress, walked to the head of the bed, pulling he went. As the mattress underneath was exposed, he saw that the dirt, the spills, and the urine had seeped through there as well. He dropped the sheet in despair, scanning the whole bed, as if seeing it for the first time. Even the wood frame, the headboard, and footboard were stained and weathered. A sticky liquid had run down the footboard near the middle and dried. The wood was cracked and worn.

He stood for a moment, wondering how this was possible. *Someone else must have done this. They broke in. I did leave the window open a few days ago. Or was that last week? I have hardly been here, I have been working so much. There is no way I would let it get to this point.* He decided to sleep downstairs on the couch.

He walked out the door, grabbed the handle, and closed it, making sure it latched shut.

So Quiet

"Did you notice anything strange about Kelly?"

Jason paused at the copying machine, checking the paper tray. "No, I don't think so. I only spoke to her briefly this morning."

"She talked to you?"

He pushed the button to begin the copies and turned to look at Ruth. "Sure. We said 'good morning' and I asked her how her trip to Kathmandu was."

"Did she answer you?"

Jason frowned. "Of course. She told me all about some ancient village up in the mountains she explored. Why?"

Ruth shook her head. "I don't know. I said good morning to her as we passed in the hall, and she completely ignored me. So later I went into her office and asked her how she was. She stopped what she was doing on her computer and just stared at the wall. Finally, I asked if she was mad at me, and she shook her head no. But she wouldn't say a word or look at me."

"Strange. Did something happen between you two?"

"Not that I know of. She was perfectly fine before she left last week. I haven't seen or talked to her until today."

"I don't know what to tell you. I didn't notice anything out of the ordinary."

"Okay. Thanks anyway, Jason. We'll get it sorted out, I'm sure." She left the copying room.

Jason pulled the copies from the tray and then the original from the scanner. He wasn't really close to either Kelly or Ruth. Both had been here for a few years, before he started. Kelly was in her 30s, and Ruth was in her 60s, so he had more in common with Kelly. They both seemed like normal people—not given to drama. Hard to imagine Kelly refusing to answer, even if she was miffed at Ruth.

He shrugged his shoulders and went back to his office.

Joseph waited for his cup of noodles to finish cooking in the microwave. He couldn't believe it was already 1:30. Busy day! But he had to get a lot done because he had an appointment at his cardiologist tomorrow. Had to do it periodically because of his arrhythmia. Infrequent, but concerning.

A noise in the room caused him to turn . It was Kelly, taking a yogurt out of the refrigerator. "Hey, Kelly! How was your trip?" She looked at him and ducked her head, and then almost ran out of the break room.

Joseph frowned. *That was strange. She's usually so friendly.*

The microwave pinged. He took out the little Styrofoam cup, grabbed a plastic spoon from the collection, and headed back to his office.

Down the hall he heard voices, and, as he passed the big conference room, he saw Kelly and Janine inside. He stuck his head in, "Hi, girls, how's it going?"

"Hi, Joseph! Good, how are you?" Janine said with a smile. "We were just talking about Kelly's trip. Sounds remarkable!"

Kelly did not look at him.

"Where did you go, Kelly?" She turned and looked at him briefly, and then looked away. She gave a rapid shake of her head, and then looked down at the floor.

Janine was visibly embarrassed at Kelly's behavior. "Uh, well, maybe I talked her ear off. So fascinating, some little village she visited, like going back to ancient times."

He smiled. "Well, I hope to hear about it eventually. Got a call to make now. See you both later." If she was irritated with him, so be it. At age 63, he cared little about what people thought.

"Hi, Ruth. Have a seat."

"Thanks for giving me a moment, boss." She took the chair in front of the desk and fidgeted with the arm. "I wanted to talk to you about Kelly."

"Kelly? If this was a problem with a coworker, you should probably talk to HR."

"No, no, it's not really a problem. I'm worried about her. Ever since she got back from her trip, she doesn't talk to people. Or rather, she talks to some people, but not others."

"What do you mean, she doesn't talk to them? At all?"

"She'll shake her head back-and-forth, but other than that, she just stares off and won't even look at them."

Damon frowned. "Did she have some argument or conflict with them?"

"None of us can think of a thing. In fact, right before she left for her trip, she had some great conversations with those same people."

"But it's not everybody?"

"No. I know she won't talk to Joseph because I saw it. Malinda said the same. But I saw her talking normally to Janine and Jacqueline, and apparently she talks to Jason."

Damon pursed his lips. "That's a little strange, but it just sounds like some personal things. Is it creating a problem with her work?"

"No. At least no one has complained about it. She does her work, sends or hands things to people. She just won't talk to us."

"And you three are the only ones?"

"As far as I know."

He drummed his fingers on the desk, silent for a minute. "I can't very well order her to start talking to people, as long as she's doing her job. Maybe she'll confront them or get over it."

Jason hung up the phone and made a few notes before turning to the next task.

As he turned back to his computer, he heard Kelly's voice down the hall. He looked up as she walked past with the new intern, Jacqueline.

"Kelly!" he called out. They both stepped back in the door frame. "Sorry to interrupt. Kelly, would you mind finding the history on the Billerbeck account for me? Just year-to-date. You've been working on it, right?"

Kelly looked uncomfortable and turned to the side. Both Jacquelyn and Jason waited.

"Kelly? Are you okay?" Jason said.

Still not looking, she gave a brief nod and looked down at the floor. Jason exchanged a look with Jacqueline, who looked puzzled.

"Kelly?"

No response. Finally, Jacqueline spoke.

"I was helping her go over it yesterday, I'm sure we can find them. Can we email you?"

"Sure…sure. Thank you both."

Jason could see the relief in her face as she turned away. *What the hell? Isn't that what Ruth was complaining about the other day? Kelly wouldn't talk to her at her, and she didn't know why. But he'd had a normal conversation with her just a few days ago.*

He shrugged and turned back to the computer.

"Hello, Kelly," Damon said. "Come on in and have a seat." He watched carefully as she ducked her head and took one of the chairs in front of his desk. She did not meet his eyes. He had known Kelly for a couple of years, and while they were not friends, they were always friendly. After all, he was her boss, and she was a good employee. Making this more difficult.

"How are you doing, Kelly?"

Still not making eye contact, she nodded her head. Damon waited, but she just kept staring at the front of his desk to the left.

"Are you sure? You don't seem to be acting like yourself."

Still nothing but a slight shake of the head.

"Very well. I will address the reason I called you here. A number of your colleagues have told me that you no longer speak to them. I want you to know that they did not come to me because they were upset or angry. They came to me because they were worried about you."

He paused, hoping for some reaction. There was none except uncomfortableness.

"Is something wrong? Did they do something that has made you not want to talk to them?"

She shook her head.

"Kelly, I am not here to reprimand you. You're an excellent worker, and you've always gotten along with everyone. So, this is a change, and I would like to know how we can help. I understand if it's something personal you might not want to discuss it, but could you at least tell me if you're having difficulties outside of work? You know we can be accommodating."

She fidgeted in the chair, rubbing her fingers together, still staring at the same spot on his desk. Again, she shook her head no.

He sighed. If she wouldn't communicate, he wasn't sure what to do. "Would you like some coffee or some water?"

She nodded.

"Coffee?"

Kelly shook her head.

"Water?"

She nodded. So, she *was* communicating, she just wouldn't speak. *Maybe she's having a problem with her voice?* he thought. *No, that doesn't make sense. She's talking to some people.* He was grasping at straws. He leaned over and pushed the intercom. "James, would you bring us a couple bottles of water?"

"Kelly, you seem very uncomfortable and that's not my intention. It's just that some of your colleagues want to know why you won't talk to them."

James knocked at the door and entered. Kelly jumped a bit and then turned and looked at him and smiled. He placed a bottle of water in front of Damon, and then handed the other to Kelly.

"Thank you, James," she said.

A perfectly normal tone. No discomfort. No awkwardness. She even smiled at James. All normal.

James nodded to both of them and left the office, closing the door. Kelly opened the bottle of water and took a long gulp, still staring at the front of the desk.

"I don't understand. You talk to James normally, but you won't talk to me. Did *I* do something to upset you? Did they do something to upset you?"

She shook her head as she fumbled to put the cap back on the bottle.

"Very well. I can see you don't want to talk to me, and that's okay. I don't know what you're dealing with, and perhaps it is personal. That is also okay. There have been no complaints about your work. But if this situation causes problems here, I will have to address the issue. Do you understand?"

Kelly nodded again. He waited, hoping she would say something when her job might be on the line, but there was nothing.

"Please know Kelly, we are concerned about you, and that's all it is. If you need to talk to me, or anyone else, please do it. Thank you for coming. You may go."

She bolted out of the seat as if it were on fire.

Damon always sat at the head of the table at these weekly meetings, with James to his right, taking notes. Others filed in and took seats as available.

He looked at his watch and turned to James. "Is everyone here? Maybe we start early and go over production figures for last month?"

James consulted his tablet. "Still waiting for Piper, Kelly, and Thomas."

"Okay." He looked around the table, then spoke loudly. "Everyone, let me have your attention. This is a little out of the ordinary, but some of you have expressed concern about Kelly. Let's talk a little. If she enters, just go back to your conversations—I don't want her to feel awkward. What are your concerns about her?"

Everyone looked around the table, waiting for someone to speak. Finally, Joseph raised a hand.

"Well, boss, it's strange. She's always been a good, friendly coworker. But she won't talk to me. Started after she got back from that exotic trip."

"Same here," Ruth said, not wanting to mention she had gone to the boss about it.

There was some fidgeting. Janine spoke next. "She was talking to me after the trip, and—"

"It isn't everyone, I know." Damon said.

"—it seemed normal. Uh, she was talking to me. Not anymore. Now she acts awkward around me and won't even look directly at."

"That's what happened with me, too," Jason said. "Perfectly normal interactions until this week."

"That's interesting." This was Aaron, the sales team leader. "She was talking to me, too. Then, the same behavior as they describe."

"Me, too!" Malinda exclaimed, usually quiet in these meetings. "Did we do something wrong ?"

This was getting interesting. "Jacqueline," Damon said, "will you go to the door and let us know when she is on her way?" Jacqueline got up and took a seat by the door, where she could see down the hallway through the open door.

"Thank you, Jacqueline. I tried talking to her last week, and she would not speak. Let me see a show of hands. Who *is* she speaking to?"

Only James and Jacqueline raised their hands. The boss frowned.

Hector, the lead engineer, spoke up. "Hold up, everyone." He looked at Joseph. "You said she wasn't talking to you when she returned from her trip?"

Joseph nodded. "Yes, I remember because I had been wanting to ask her about the trip. It sounded so unusual."

"It was the same with me," Ruth said. "Nothing since she got back, even when I asked her about the trip."

Hector scribbled on a notepad. "But she stopped talking to the others later on?"

The rest, except for James and Jacqueline, nodded in affirmation.

Hector nodded. "Interesting. Okay, let's try this—"

Jacqueline interrupted. "She's coming."

Some started talking to their neighbor, while others looked at papers. Kelly and Piper entered the conference room, in conversation. Piper placed on hand on Kelly's arm as she was talking and said, "Morning, everyone. Thomas is on the call with Phillips Tech, said he'd be here as soon as possible."

"Excellent, thank you," Damon said. The two women sat next to each other in two of the remaining five seats. He noted that Kelly chose to sit between Piper and Jacqueline, even though there was the closer seat was between Piper and Joseph. "Let's get started. I don't have a lot today, but let's go over all the department statuses from last month and then the figures."

"Good work, everyone. We're staying on target. I'll call the meeting adjourned, but I'd Ike the department leaders to stay for a bit. The rest of you don't need to be here. Thank you." Everyone left except Joseph, Malinda, Aaron, Jason, Janine, and James. The boss turned to James. "You stay, too."

After the others had left, Damon turned to Hector. "What were you going to say before Kelly and Piper came in?" Hector was a brilliant engineer with a penchant for spotting details and patterns that others usually missed.

Hector flipped back to his notes, scanning them. "An idea…may I ask more questions?"

"Of course."

"If you all can look at your calendars and, the best you can, tell me when Kelly stopped talking to you."

Everyone nodded and began scrolling through their devices. Soon, they began relaying the information to Hector, who wrote the information on a large legal pad which he had turned sideways. They sat silently as he continued to work. Eventually, he spoke while still looking down at his notes. "This is interesting. And strange."

"Don't keep us in suspense, Hector," Damon said.

"First, I need to ask each of you your age."

Most of them frowned at the strange request, but complied. After about five more minutes of writing and scribbling, he set down the mechanical pencil and looked up. "Okay. I cannot tell you why. But there is an intriguing pattern when you correlate time and ages. When Kelly returned from her trip, she was not speaking to Ruth or Joseph, but, as far as we know, she was speaking to everyone else."

"Why just us?" Ruth said.

"The next week, she stopped talking to Aaron and Malinda. Around the third week, she no longer would speak to Jason or Damon."

He stopped, checking his paper.

"I don't see any pattern. What does—"

"Oh, wow," Janine exclaimed. You're saying it's our age. And getting younger."

"Age? Whatever do you mean?" Ruth said.

Hector looked back up. "The first week, she did not speak to people in their sixties. Then fifties. Later, forties, then thirties. Each phase lasted about a week."

"That makes no sense," Damon said.

"And today," Hector continued, "She was speaking to Piper when she came in. Piper is 29. She spoke to Jacqueline, who is 27. She stopped talking to Janine last week, who is 38.

They all sat silent for a moment, thinking back over the last few weeks with expressions of confusion. Damon recalled how, in his office, Kelly wouldn't speak to him, age 49, but she was friendly with James, who is 23.

"You're saying that she is refusing to speak to younger and younger people?" Jason said. "Why would she do that?"

"As I said, I'm just pointing out the pattern. I have no data that would indicate the reason."

"She's doing it on *purpose*?"

Damon spoke again. "Okay, it's a pattern. Pretty solid pattern. What we don't know is if she is doing it deliberately, and if so, why."

"Of *course* she's doing it on purpose. There's no other explanation." That was Aaron.

"Well, I don't know…" Ruth said. "Think about Tourette's Syndrome. Or narcolepsy. Those are neurological disorders that *can* seem like a person is doing it on purpose."

"I've never heard of anything like this," Aaron replied.

Damon leaned forward. "Just because we haven't heard of it doesn't mean it doesn't exist."

Aaron looked taken aback. "Well, okay. But it doesn't mean she *isn't* doing it on purpose."

"True," Damon said. "So, what *reasons* might she have for doing this?"

Silence. He waited.

"You know…" Ruth said, "dementia is sort of like this. A person slowly becomes more and more like a child. My mother—"

"Yeah, but not like this."

"I'm not saying it's dementia. Maybe something like it. Regression."

Hector was still writing something, but spoke again as he wrote. "Where did she go on her trip?"

"Kathmandu. Major trip she's been planning for years. Wanted to see some old village up in the mountains she read about."

The boss gestured with his arm. "Okay, people, our goal is to help her, not diagnose her. She's still talking to people under thirty? So maybe one of them should talk to her now, before she won't speak to them, and see if they get anywhere."

"I'd be glad to do it," Piper said. "I've always gotten along with her."

"Hey, Kelly? You got a moment? I wanted to introduce you to my daughter, Camille." Janine entered Kelly's office with the young girl behind her.

Kelly stood up. "Hi, Camille," she said, avoiding any acknowledgment of Janine. "Nice to meet you. Are you enjoying our special day here at work?"

"Hi, Miss Kelly. Yes. I came to bring-your-child day last year. So much fun seeing what mom does."

"I think what you like is the donuts in the break room," Janine laughed, knowing Kelly would not look at her or speak. But she *was* talking to a 12-year-old.

"Well, Camille, if it's okay with your mom, I actually have some donuts here. Would you like one?"

Interesting. thought Janine. *She will refer to me, but not acknowledge I am right here.*

Camille looked at her mom. "Can I?"

"Of course, dear." She looked over. "Thank you, Kelly."

No answer or even a glance.

At that moment, Piper knocked on the door. "Sorry to interrupt. I see we have one of our visitors." Janine introduced her to Camille.

After welcoming Camille, Piper turned to Kelly. "Do you have time for lunch today? Love to catch up—to hear more about your trip!"

Kelly sat down and looked at her desk, unresponsive and awkward. Piper looked at Janine and shook her head in dismay.

She sat on the floor of her apartment, wearing only a baggy pair of shorts. A juice box lay on its side beside her. She was so tired from the day. A nap was needed, but she didn't want to. Maybe she could get a blanket and pillow though, and lay down in front of the TV.

She grabbed a handful of Cheerios from a bowl beside her and crammed them in her mouth. Looking up at the TV, which was playing an old Bugs Bunny cartoon, she laughed. A few of the Cheerios fell out, joining some other stray toruses on the floor.

She wrinkled her nose. It smelled bad in here! A cackle escaped her lips.

Shrugging, she picked up the little toy next to her. Turning it over, she ran her finger along the rough surface. It looked like a dried up reptile or an enormous dried insect. She smiled when she remembered the old man who gave it to her when she was in the village.

It was her favorite toy ever. She began to cry.

So Alive

Walking wobbly on the beach of smooth sand, footprints trailing behind. Warm air and gentle breeze cools my skin like a tiny kitten tottering past. A seaweed forest of verdant vegetation, the shadows hiding hive-like mysteries, lies ahead. I feel it. Something soft but seen not. More than physical but not quite psychological.

The humid air and stillness are an oppressing blanket thrown atop it all. Swish, crack, snap accompanies me. Drip drip drop as I disturb the moisture resting atop the fronds from the fresh morn. The ground rises, my legs pump pump pump with added effort; my breath puff puff puffs.

I stand as a statue at the exposed substratum of a rocky hill, gazing at the summit cone, topped with ice cream snow. The clouds and a sky made of lapis lazuli beckon like an alluring woman. I hunger for her.

Climbing crab crab up the slope, my arms are balancing wings, the mystery of gravity and locomotion in a ludic gyration. My breath and heartbeat working together are a small engine revving up.

I stand at the summit, unable to appreciate the presence of the precipice beyond, my lungs a baby protesting the insufficiency of air, my muscles a newborn calf.

Recovering, I creak to vertical, hip-holding hands as I smile a smile of success. Small success. Dun I, they say: this mountain is Dun I. I do not fathom but it fits.

Dun I.

He used to climb here come the morning. Mourning his land, lamenting his island. On the clearest of days, he could discern it. A dark stroke atop of the sea, sitting serenely, even without him. Perhaps because it was without him.

A green emerald loved and lost. His calling had with a clan—a clan of clans not of this world. A scribe. Cutting, rolling, creasing, dipping, writing, copying. Beautiful ligatures beckoned literature of bountiful eloquence. But not merely expressiveness. There was meaning, purpose, life. Ultimate significance, objective existence. His purpose was to provide for posterity with his pen and his piety.

Sacred duplication for preservation. He required a roll from a related clan. They refused! A riddle. A resentment. A wrong.

Such work should not be hindered. Like Abram, he took on matters himself. They demanded. He refused. The mission must be maintained.

But blind faith turns grace to grasping. Humility to hubris. It was a brutal battle for the book. No mere book, true. But not worth three thousand lives. Brothers betrayed to a burial.

Sometimes, revelation requires ruination.

I scuffled up to the stone seat he had shaped by stacking rocks. I climbed and sat, just as he had sat centuries ago. Not with the same longing, not with the same lament. Yet I have my own craving, my own contrition. He and I are *anamcara* in this moment.

Long ago, summoned, he stood, eyes sideways, shoulders slumped. Recompense must be paid, but penance may bring peace. But the summoner said no. The extent of egregiousness requires exile.

All those centuries ago, he raised his head. "I will build a bastion across the sea, and I will rescue three thousand in payment of the three thousand who perished."

So he sailed, plying the sea to this place. Twelve and one they were, rowing oars and working sails. Then, a beam of brightness illuminated the island. "This is the place."

I stand. Down the mountain, at the base of Dun I, I see the stone buildings, the stone hut, the simple poustinia, and the skyward monuments. From here they set out for the coast, seeking converts.

The wind picks up; I wind my peacoat around me. Such stubbornness and single-mindedness turned to slaughter. But the result was a remarkable hinge in history.

I make my way down the stone incline. The lowing of cattle. The bleating of sheep. The lapping of waves. The whistle of the wind. It is all peace now, a tiny island wrought from misguided faith, murder, exile, building, destruction, more death, a rebuilding, and finally, a renewal.

It is a lesson of life. Haughtiness to humility. Life from loss. Anguish to aspiration.

Dry bones came to life on a tiny island, and the world was changed.

AFTERWORD

The idea for this collection of short stories came from my love of languages. I was doing some reading of an ancient Greek manuscript, and became fascinated by the use of adverbs, and how they were employed. It got me to thinking about adverbs in English, and how English grammar can be perplexing: "English is not a language, it is three languages wearing a trench coat pretending to be one."[2]

The word "so" came to my mind. I knew from teaching languages that this tiny word causes many problems for new English speakers, as well as for translators. The word can have six different uses in English.

1. It can indicate a consequence, similar to the word "therefore." "It was raining today, so I stayed inside." This is called a conjunctive adverb or a coordinating conjunction.

2. It can indicate a purpose, as in "in order that." "I put sugar in my coffee, so it would be sweet." This is called a subordinating conjunction.

3. It can indicate addition, similar to "and also." "I take my coffee black; so does my girlfriend. " This is known as a conjunctive adverb, and it often introduces a second clause.

4. It can express confirmation or agreement. In this use, it will typically follow a question. "Did you set out the garbage today?" "I think so." This makes it a strange

---

[2]Attributed to Gugulethu Mhlungu.

word. It's not a pronoun in the strict sense because it refers back to the entire question or statement. It's really a substitute word for the previous question or statement.

5. There are some strange uses of "so" that do not fit into any of the regular categories. I suppose these would be labeled idioms or idiomatic phrases. "So! You are the one who left the dishes out." "I'm feeling somewhat so-so today."

6. Finally, it can intensify another word, similar to the use of "very." "It is so windy today." This makes it function as an adverb that qualifies as an adjective (in the above sentence, "so" intensifies the adjective "windy.") It is a bit different from "very," because it usually indicates a high degree of intensification.

One of the major themes in my writings is chaos. I enjoy exploring how people respond to loss, external issues that overwhelm them, actions of their own that snowball out of control, and so on. We all feel overwhelmed sometimes, or we feel like the world is against us, or everything is going wrong, or we just can't get ahead. It's a wonderful theme to explore the human condition. I always hope my readers are entertained, but also ask themselves what would I do in this situation?

Therefore, I chose the last usage of "so"— high intensification of an adjective. **"So Dense"** is a story about a scientifically unknown fog bank that envelops a city, and a blind woman who seems to know more than the climate scientists. (This is also a bit of irony: the blind can see, while the sighted do not understand.)

"So Humane" is the story of the "louisette"—or, as is more commonly known, the "guillotine." The background of the story is historically accurate. Antoine Louis, a physiolo-

gist and surgeon, along with a German engineer named To-
bias Schmidt, built the first device. On October 10, 1789,
French physician and Freemason Joseph-Ignace Guillotin, a
death penalty opponent, formally proposed that the device be
used for executions because it would be more humane, in
line with the ideals of human rights during the Enlighten-
ment period. His proposal persuaded King Louis XVI of
France to make it so. Guillotin's name became an eponym
for the device.[3] My idea was to write a story about the very
first person executed using this device: a man not only facing his own death, but the unknown of how it would happen.

"So Kind" is an exploration of how modern-day men and
women have such a difficult time finding a romantic partner,
and how such a desire might lead us to overlook problematic
issues, merely because someone is "so kind." It's possible
for someone to act kind and be evil at the same time. Humans are complex.

"So Long" is a story that came from an experience I had
while traveling through the countryside by train in northern
Italy. It is not uncommon for desperate people to commit
suicide by jumping in front of a high-speed train. I was traveling in such a train, and it stopped in the middle of the
countryside. No announcement was made apart from that we
would be paused in the countryside for a while. Unlike in the
US, where the police would keep anyone from entering the
scene, I was able to walk to the front of the train. I assumed
we had mechanical trouble, or had hit an abandoned item

---

[3]It originally had a curved blade, but the memoirs of the famous
French executioner, Charles-Henri Sanson, tell us that the
King wanted a straight angle blade instead of the curved blade,
which became common. The *last* person executed in the Western world legally by the guillotine was a murderer named
Hamida Djandoubi, on September 10, 1977. The death penalty
was outlawed in France in 1981.

placed on the tracks, or, at worst, had struck an animal. Needless to say, it was a bit traumatic for me, and it eventually led me to wonder what would lead a person to dive in front of a train going 180 km an hour.

"So Rude" came from a discussion I had with some friends about how some people who seem extremely rude might actually have something traumatic going on in their life. Perhaps they would rather not be rude, but they cannot help themselves because there is so much pain. Maybe they want to avoid facing the fact that they have trauma, so they keep trying to pretend to be nice when they really would like to take their anger out on someone else. It's a sad commentary on how we judge one another, without knowing the full story—all too common in today's America.

"So Snowy" was a challenge presented to me one Christmas Eve by a friend. It was my first Christmas alone after my wife divorced me to marry another man. I always enjoyed Christmas, yet here I was feeling so alone and depressed. I sat at a mall, watching all the activity by couples and families. As I texted with my friend about my mood, she said, "Write a story for me about Christmas. Right now." So, I went to the food court, sat down at a table with a Christmas drink, and wrote "So Snowy."

"So Sweet" is a story about the ravages of losing your mind as we grow older. Alzheimer's and dementia are difficult diseases, like many, I have experienced it in grandparents and others. Yet, at the same time, I would like to believe that small, hopeful, almost magical things can happen in our lives, to give us a little joy in the midst of the pain, suffering, and loss.

"So Tired" also came out of the period where I was experiencing depression and grief, as many do after a major loss. As most of us know, great losses can cause us fall into a pattern of just going through the motions of life. A common thread among depressed people is that they stay in bed a lot, and live a life of what Thoreau called "quiet desperation."[4] Going through the motions of work, life, home, and all the other things we do, just because we don't know what else to do with our lives. And slowly, that life can become black-and-white, meaningless, and utterly decrepit. What would you do if you found yourself in this character's place?

The story, "**So Quiet**," came from an event that a friend related to me. A coworker or teacher at a school had suddenly stopped talking to the adults. He had no trouble talking to children, but could not (or would not) speak to adults. This fascinated me, and led to writing a story about what might happen in this situation (with a twist added by me, of course) and why. An underlying theme is also the tragedy of losing one's mind, as in "So Sweet."

"**So Alive**" is an attempt to end this collection of short stories by moving beyond chaos to hope, and perhaps, even joy. It is based on some history I learned on a trip to the Isle of Iona (off the coast of the western highlands in Scotland). In the 6th century AD, an Irish monk named Columba was ex-iled for his role in a war between rival monasteries over a manuscript which he refused to return. (Really!) Over 3,000 men were killed. Upon his sentence to exile, he repented, and said that he would go away and found a monastery, and

---

[4]"The mass of men lead lives of quiet desperation. What is called resignation is confirmed desperation. From the desper-ate city you go into the desperate country, and have to console yourself with the bravery of minks and muskrats. A stereo-typed but unconscious despair is concealed even under what are called the games and amusements of mankind. There is no play in them, for this comes after work. But it is a characteris-tic of wisdom not to do desperate things.." (Henry David Thoreau, *Civil Disobedience and Other Essays*.)

bring 3,000 people to Christ as redemption. He sailed with a few others, and landed on Iona, and built a monastery. There, he was responsible (among others) for the Christianization of Scotland. After I climbed Dun I on Iona, I wrote this as a quasi-stream of consciousness a piece on my journey, imagining what Saint Columba experienced as he walked on the little island so long ago.

Language is the most direct and effective manner of communication in connection with fellow humans.[5] Our actions, gestures, and expressions are mere support for verbal or written transmission. And yet, even language can be a barrier to a true connection with others. It is slippery, it is confusing, and it is open to misinterpretation—and yet it is the best we have.

I hope you find the stories entertaining and engaging, and perhaps they even made you think a bit. (Here's a bonus: did you notice how many times the word "so" is used in this afterward?)

Thank you for reading.

---

[5] While it is often said that "a picture paints 1000 words," visual communication is still not as direct and effective as the written or spoken word—especially when there is give-and-take.

About the Author

If you feel generous and have a couple of minutes, please leave a review. It makes a huge difference to me. Thank you in advance.

You can also support Markus on Patreon at
https://www.patreon.com/AuthorMarkusMcDowell

Visit his website at
https://markusmcdowell.com

You can also follow the author on social media
Instagram: https://www.instagram.com/doctormarkus_author/
Twitter: https://twitter.com/markusmcdowell
FaceBook: https://www.facebook.com/MarkusMcDowellAuthor/
Amazon Author Page: https://www.amazon.com/author/markusm-cdowell

About the Publisher

Sulis International Press publishes select fiction and non-fiction in a variety of genres under four imprints: Riversong Books, Sulis Academic Press, Sulis Press, and Keledei Publications.

For more, visit the website at
https://sulisinternational.com

Subscribe to the newsletter at
https://sulisinternational.com/subscribe/

Follow on social media
https://www.facebook.com/SulisInternational
https://twitter.com/Sulis_Intl
https://www.pinterest.com/Sulis_Intl/
https://www.instagram.com/sulis_international/